ALLI'S GIFT

KATHLEEN BURNS DENNISTON

Cover art created by Maggie Denniston and Joshua Merow
Formatting by Polgarus Studio

You sent a dragonfly to remind me that we are never apart

Love lasts forever, you can feel it in your heart.

Dedicated my angels, Elizabeth, Jamie and Maggie

Two years ago (although it seems like yesterday)

Nana, does heaven smell like the beach? I shut my eyes and let my mind wander on the warm ocean breeze.

"Alison Collins." Mom's whisper jarred me back to reality. She furrowed her brows and gave a sideways nod toward the priest standing over my grandmother's grave.

"Sorry," I whispered and turned toward the priest and the sea of black coats and dresses.

Today we could have gone clam diggin'. My face tilted toward the August sun, I inhaled the salty air of Gloucester, Massachusetts. My sister Lisa and I spent two weeks every summer here with Nana at the beach. We would run along the water's edge, letting our toes disappear in the doughy sand while Nana followed with a bucket.

How can I go on without you? A deep, choking sadness squeezed my insides. Nana was the first person I knew who had died. At twelve, I'd never even thought about death until the phone rang last week. Losing Nana was the worst feeling, so deep and raw. As if I'd never laugh again.

Dad stood in front of me and let go of Lisa's eight-year-old hand to cover his face as he shook with grief. Watching him, I got the same hollow feeling I had this morning at Nana's house. Lisa and I had been in the kitchen eating bacon and eggs, just like always, except Nana wasn't there. Silence bounced off of the walls. I needed Dad to rub my hair and wink at me, to tell me everything was going to be okay, but he didn't. He walked by me and stared out the window watching the ocean, or the tide or maybe nothing

1

at all. Mom had spoken to him in soft whispers, coaxing him to get dressed.

Lisa turned from the priest and looked at Mom, lost, but Mom just twirled her finger, signaling Lisa to turn around. Lisa glanced at me, and then turned back and held on to the bottom of Dad's suit jacket.

Dad's father died when he was a boy, and it was just Dad and Nana growing up. Nana called Dad "her baby," and it was kind of embarrassing how she always mentioned to random strangers at the store or church that Dad had made something of his life. "That boy of mine got out. Seein' the worhld." She would shake her head, like she couldn't believe it. Another favorite was, "Did you know Walta, *my* Walta, is an officca in the Ahmy?" She would boast about our townhouse in dusty, flat Ft. Riley, Kansas, making it sound like a castle, somewhere in the middle of heaven. Hardly.

Nana's house was my idea of heaven. I woke every morning to the foamy tide dancing on the sand and to the smell of breakfast cooking in the kitchen. After an afternoon on the beach, Lisa and I would race for some treat that was in the freezer. Every night, I opened the window, and drifted to sleep listening to the surf laced with the tangy smell of the sea.

Lisa and I had been taking turns marking days off the calendar since summer break began, desperate for the day we would leave for Gloucester. We only had ten more days without big red Xs in them when we got the call. Nana had died in her sleep.

Tears spilled off my cheeks as I stared at the lush grass of

St. Mary's cemetery. "I wish I had a chance to say goodbye," I whispered. "I love you, Nana."

I heard a faint sound over my right shoulder. A dragonfly swayed back and forth, so close I could see through its delicate blue and purple wings. I kept still, mesmerized by the iridescent colors glistening in the sun. Then, it hit me. The colors of the dragonfly's wings were the same gauzy purple and blue of Nana's favorite dress. The one she was buried in. My heart pounded and I held my breath watching the dragonfly. After a few seconds, it gracefully floated away into the dappled shadows of the birch trees.

"Goodbye," I whispered.

Chapter 1

"You look like a dead worm." I stared at myself in the mirror on the last morning of summer vacation. I swear three more zits had popped out on my forehead overnight. At fourteen, my body was a cruel joke, and nothing was going to make things better before tomorrow—the first day of high school. The thought of it made my stomach flip and tighten into a knot, so I flopped back onto my worn pink sheets. I'd grown two inches over the summer, my knees looked like bowling balls stuck in the middle of toothpicks, and *things* were popping out all over, mainly on my face. Add braces and stringy brown hair, and that was the sum total of my wormy good looks. Not even my new jeans and shirt from Forever 21 were going to help. On the bright side, Dad told me that I was blessed with Nana's olive skin, and I really did get tanned, unlike Lisa, who burned in the shade. Dad called me his "Native Princess," so even though I felt like a zit-faced worm, Dad made me feel good.

Margot Williamson, my official BFF, thought she had it worse. As if. She had porcelain-clear skin; bouncy, beautiful, blonde hair; and a fantastic athlete's body. All the same, she was convinced her nose, as she put it, "hung off her face like a baboon's butt." It's not huge and doesn't look anything like a baboon's butt. Okay, her nose might be kind of *unique,* but I thought it made her very pretty. She said I was full of crap.

Whenever she came over, Dad called out, "Hey there, beautiful!" and Margot turned a pretty pink color, like a Necco candy heart. She always told me I was really lucky to have a great Dad, probably because her real dad left her and her mom when she was three. Margot never really knew her real dad, but she looked a lot like him. I'd seen pictures, and she joked that her nose was the only thing her real dad ever gave her. Bill was her dad now. After he married Margot's mom, he adopted her, but Margot refused to call him dad. So she calls him Bill and the whole dad thing was a sore subject, unless she was talking about mine.

I met Margot a year ago, on the first day we arrived in Springfield, Virginia, from Kansas. She walked up to me when I was wheeling my bike off the moving van and handed me a plate of brownies. "My mom made me bring you these. I'm Margot. It rhymes with Fargo." She informed me she was going into the eighth grade. Although she seemed pretty pushy, I was glad to know someone my age. And guess what—I never once noticed her nose.

Eighth grade was my first time going to a public school, and it was terrible, no worse; it was scarring and devastating. It was, in fact, monumentally horrible, and tomorrow was high school, and there was every chance that it could, should and would be much, much worse. I had vampire bats, not butterflies, in my stomach.

Today is Labor Day. Fun. Refocus, Alli.

Great. Now, I sound like Mom.

Margot and I planned to spend the day at the pool, and then our families were going out for crabs at Cantler's in Annapolis. I was psyched. I had heard about this place on the Food Channel. I rolled off my bed and grabbed my bikini top from under the desk chair. It was still damp from yesterday's swim. "Cripes!" The cold top shocked my very sensitive areas, if you get my message. Nerp city. I pulled on the bikini bottoms, covered the suit with shorts and a T-shirt and headed downstairs.

I walked into the kitchen and spied Dad on the back deck through the sliding glass door. Sweat speckled the front of his T-shirt as he buffed his army boots. The heat here was worse than Kansas. The humidity was a killer. It felt like you were suffocating under a steamy wool blanket in the middle of a jungle. Yes, totally, exactly like that. I poured a bowl of cereal and went out to see him.

"Hey, Walt. That looks like quite a workout." I sat down in the shade and shoveled cereal in my mouth. Thankfully, our backyard was shaded by trees that included the loud, constant hum of locusts.

"Don't call me Walt, Alli. It's unsettling." He smiled, but I thought he looked tired.

"All right, jeez. Margot calls her dad Bill. I thought we could have a mature relationship now that I'm heading into the big time, high school."

He stopped buffing and raised his eyebrows. "It's not the same thing. Anyway, you don't want to be my little princess anymore?" I slid my arms around his neck and kissed his rough cheek, inhaling boot polish.

"Watch the boots!" He laughed.

"I don't know what I was thinking, Walt."

"Again with the Walt."

"Going to the pool today? There's a cookout this afternoon." I went back to my cereal and tried to keep the milk in my mouth instead of down my top.

"Nah, I'm gonna see if I can get a deal on a lawn mower. I want to do that before we leave with the Williamsons." He took a long sigh. "I hope I feel better before we go."

"What's wrong?" I tipped the bowl to get to sugary milk at the bottom.

"Is there any milk left?" Lisa poked her head out of the door.

"Let me look in the fridge with my X-ray vision." I squinted toward the brick wall.

"Oh, ha, ha, ha." She slid the door shut.

It was a genetic mystery how Lisa—with her blonde, curly hair, blue eyes and freckles—and I came from the same parents. I was the first in the batch—you know, the tester. Like that first crappy pancake, it doesn't quite work out right, but the second one is always a winner. I actually overheard Mom on the phone one day saying Lisa was "just adorable" and then in her next breath she whispered, "Alli's going through a stage." Can you believe that? It's nice to know that my mother agrees with my stupid mirror and broadcasts it to everyone. So much for maternal instincts.

Lisa couldn't wait for school to start tomorrow; she got Mrs. Bealor as her fifth grade teacher. She's been floating on cloud nine since she found out that she would have the nicest teacher at Huntsman Elementary. She pranced around the house singing how fun fifth grade was going to be; I wanted to smack the freckles off her face.

"Boy, I'm drained. I can't believe this humidity." Dad stood to go inside.

"You okay?" I asked. "You look tired."

He smirked and rubbed his arm. "Me? Super Dad?"

I followed him inside and a trickle of sweat seeped through my T-shirt. "Lisa, stay inside, it's oppressive out there."

"Whatever," Lisa mumbled from the refrigerator.

I used every opportunity to demonstrate to Lisa that I was older and wiser. Mom called Virginia's heat *oppressive*. I didn't know what it meant, but I figured it was something like, *it's so dang hot; it's impressive.*

"Mom, I'm going to Margot's and then the pool," I yelled.

"Alli?" I heard footsteps cross the floor above me. "Be home at three o'clock to get ready to go out."

"Roger that!" I said in my best army-brat form. I grabbed my pool bag and headed out the door. It was sizzling outside, so I tore off my T-shirt as soon as I got on my bike. Margot lived about ten houses away, or twenty-two seconds on my bike. I felt kind of like a nerd riding my bike—my knees hit the handle bars when I pedaled—but it was like a microwave outside and pretty much a downhill glide to Margot's house.

As I turned onto the sidewalk, I saw *My God Matt* Thomas, or as Margot and I called him MGM, mowing his lawn. Margot and I seriously needed a code so we could talk about him and no one would know, because every time we heard him or heard someone talking about the twelfth grade miracle, we melted into giggling fools. Unfortunately for me, Matt had a younger sister, Cheryl—the reason eighth grade had been a social disaster. Cheryl was the pack leader of the wolves at West Springfield Junior High. I was the new kid on the block. Fresh meat. I practically skipped into the wolf's den on that first day of school. I didn't even know who Cheryl was when I walked into eighth grade English. All I did was innocently trip over a backpack on my way to sharpen my pencil. That turned out to be my permanent fall from grace.

"You okay, Spaz?" Cheryl had said. Everyone howled with laughter. From that moment on I was "Spaz." Cheryl pounced on any chance to humiliate me, trip me, push me into the lockers—anything to make my life a living hell. You know that feeling when you have to go to the doctor, and you know you're getting a shot? Well, that's what I felt like every morning last year. The whole year was torture, and at the end of it, I threw out my yearbook because everyone's entry started, "Dear Spaz."

The only reason I survived was because of Margot and her nerves of steel. Margot protected me from Cheryl as much as she could, and when she couldn't, well, she swore like a sailor. (Nana used to say that.) Margot's mom was always grounding her for swearing, mainly because she swore very loudly—about Cheryl. As a result, we developed the Alternative to Swearing List or ASL. It was created this past spring, and I'm proud to say Margot's only been grounded four times since—for swearing, that is. I thought up most of the words; Margot thought up the examples.

The List of Acceptable Words for Young Ladies/Alternative to Swearing List
(Or words that Elaine can't ground Margot for saying.)

Festering foot fungus (3F)

Cheryl's outfit looks like 3F.

Sewer Manure

You smell like Sewer Manure, or your face looks like sewer manure. (Alli's dad especially likes this one.)

Beelzebub's bosom buddy (3B)

You're a 3B, straight up.

Vomitosa

Cheryl Thomas looks like hot pile of Vomitosa.

Buck-toothed trollop (this and 3B are the worst to be called.)

Cheryl is a buck-toothed trollop. (Margot's personal favorite.)

Addendum (Words that need to be invented, seriously.)

Terrorment

When I look at MGM, I tremble with terrorment.

Thrillified

When I go on a rollercoaster, I'm thrillified.

I was seriously thrillified as I pedaled closer to the Thomases' house—partly because 3B might be lurking around, but mainly because MGM was only wearing shorts. His brown wavy hair fell over his forehead, sweat glistened on his body and his shorts were low enough to see his (gulp) boxers and tan line. Simply a god. The sweet smell of MGM's perfectly cut grass met me as I approached their house.

"Hey Matt," I called over the sound of the mower.

He wiped the hair from his eyes and gave a quick nod.

I raised my hand in casual friendliness, and my bike swerved, causing the front tire to jam into the edge of the sidewalk. I tried to gain control by yanking the handlebars in the opposite direction, and the strap of my pool bag fell off my shoulder and caught on the hand-brake, jerking the handlebars yet again. I bounced off my bike, hit the curb and splattered on the street, like a heap of road kill. Invisible huge hands squeezed my lungs. Couldn't breathe.

"Hey! Are you okay?" Matt ran across the yard and knelt beside me.

I grabbed his arm and stared at him, my mouth gaping. My life's goal became taking a breath.

"Alli! Take it easy. It's okay." He put his hand on my shoulder.

I looked at his tan, sweating body, and Death's hands let go of my lungs. The world came back in focus and I sucked in.

"Oh—oh my God," came out in a shaky voice. *Now that I can breathe, please let me die.*

12

"It's okay." He rubbed my arm gently. "You had the wind knocked out of you. You'll be okay. Here, try and get up." His warm, firm hand steadied me. As I leaned on Matt, I glanced into the blinding sunshine and saw the silhouette of a dragonfly floating gracefully over his head. I couldn't believe how weird that was, but my eyes were back to MGM's bare chest that smelled like coconut suntan lotion. *You are so perfect.*

Pain shot down my calf. I looked down at a bloody mess of black pebbles stuck to raw skin. *No! Don't do it.* I bit my lip and looked up. The dragonfly was still there. *Do not cry.* I blurted, "Thanks Matt." My leg throbbed as I teetered to find my balance.

"Uh, that's okay. Man, you better go take care of that," Matt quickly glanced away like something was very interesting across the street. Still looking away, he swiped his hand across his chest, like wiping sweat off or something.

I glanced down at myself. "Ohhh," I moaned. Flashing like a neon sign, my underdeveloped, pink and white boob had popped out of my bikini top. I made another moan that sounded more like a dying dog and pulled the top back over my now nerping boob. I sucked in my breath and clenched my teeth shut to keep from screaming.

Matt knit his brows and pursed his lips as if in pain.

I shouldn't have held my breath, because I had no control of what shot out as I gasped for air. A combination of spit, snot and dignity flew out of my mouth at the same time. I covered my face and shook my head. "I'm so sorry," I mumbled through my hand. Then, I smacked my knee on

13

the handle bar as I got on my bike and let out another hideous snort.

"It's okay…or um, no problem." Matt let me pass.

I looked back as I rode past him, and there, standing in their doorway, was Cheryl. She stared at me while her mouth moved non-stop into her cell phone.

Chapter 2

By the time I got to Margot's, blood stained my leg while tears and snot covered my face. Margot stood up from weeding the flower bed. "Alli! What happened?"

"Only the end of my life." I wiped my nose with my hand and told her the ghastly story.

"This could be the seriously worst thing I have ever heard."

Fresh tears stung my eyes.

"I mean, *oh my God*, he seriously saw your boob? Did he touch it, you know, by accident? He didn't try to touch it, did he?"

"What! No. I mean, yes. He saw it; he didn't touch it. God, Margot. What a thing to say!"

"Well, by accident, you know, he could have." Margot shook her head in disbelief. "And Cheryl saw?"

"I don't know how much she saw, but she was already blabbing about it to someone when I was leaving." My head and leg throbbed.

"Well," she squinted at my leg and looked disgusted at

the situation, my leg or both. "That's not good."

Good observation, Einstein. "Everyone in the world will know about this by tomorrow," I said.

"Don't worry about that bucked-toothed trollop. Let's go clean you up." She opened the door. "Elaine! Alli's hurt!" Margot is also on a first name basis with her mother unless she's really in the dumps, then it is Mom. I've suggested therapy.

Mrs. Williamson came down the stairs. "Lord, Alli. What happened?"

"I fell off my bike."

"In front of the Thomases' house," Margot said. Then she smirked and added, "Matt Thomas saw her boob."

Mrs. Williamson looked at me with wide eyes.

I nodded. "Somehow my suit got caught on my bike." My eyes watered up, and I pointed down to my leg. "See where I fell?"

"Mercy! What an ordeal." She came over and gave me a hug. Mrs. Williamson had what she called "big bones" and her hugs were cushy and comforting.

"Alli, did you call your mom?"

"No. I left my phone at home."

"Okay, you girls go to the bathroom. I'll be up after I call Alli's Mom." Mrs. Williamson reached for the phone.

We went into the bathroom at the top of the stairs and Margot's little sister, June, came in.

"Gross! What happened?"

"Get out, butt-face. Mom! June's bugging us," Margot yelled.

"Uh, I fell off my bike. It really hurts," I said.

"There, now you know. Now seriously, get lost," Margot said.

"Jeez, Margot. She's just seven. She's curious."

June was another touchy subject with Margot. June was really her half sister; Bill and Mrs. Williamson had June together. June was really cute with short, brown hair and blue eyes. She didn't look anything like Margot (she looked like Bill with a button nose), and well, I think you can see how this might be a sore subject.

Mrs. Williamson entered the bathroom. "I told your mom I'd clean you up. I just finished that emergency care class that I took for school. Who knew it would come in so handy?" She patted my back and sat next to me on the edge of the tub. "Still going to the pool?" she asked.

"I don't think I want to go in the water," I said through clenched teeth. "That *really* hurts."

"Elaine! Are you trying to kill her?"

"Sorry, Alli." She smiled at me and then looked sternly at Margot. "You have to get all the pebbles out. Change the subject."

"Well, we could go to the pool just for a burger or something," Margot said.

"You'd stay out of the water for me?" I gripped the side of the tub.

"Well, no. But I'd tell you how refreshing and cool the water feels if you want."

"Okay, that should do it." Mrs. Williamson covered my entire calf with gauze.

"Okay, the pool's out. Come on, I'll walk your bike home for you," Margot said as I limped behind her.

"Thanks, Mrs. Williamson." I shuffled toward the door.

"See you tonight," she said.

"Let's walk down a block and then cut over to your house. That way we'll skip the scene of the crime." Margot nudged me with her elbow and smiled.

"Thanks, Marg." I tried to think of an excuse not to go to school tomorrow. "Maybe I can pretend to get my period and have crippling cramps," I said. "My mom won't make me go to school if I tell her that."

"Nah, that won't work. You would have to produce some kind of *evidence*." She made air quotation marks with her fingers. "Anyway, MGM is a senior now. I don't think your boobs are really *big* news." She cupped her hands in front of herself, faking Dolly Parton size knockers. "Besides, I bet 3B just saw the wipe out."

My leg felt sore and something was sticking to the gauze. "What could be worse than this?" The locusts hummed loudly as we walked in the boiling mid-day sun. "I'm ruined."

"Hey, Alli, I've got your back. Seriously. No one will say anything to you." Margot had serious *chutzpah* as Nana would say. She told people what she thought right to their face, unlike me, who avoided confrontation like a frightened rabbit. "Have you noticed Cheryl's front teeth are looking more and more fangled? She's starting to look like Austin Powers and Bugs Bunny's love child."

"That's pretty funny."

"Gwoowvy Baby." Her lispy British accent actually made me crack up. Margot always seemed to be there when I needed her. Last year she had seen Cheryl push me in the cafeteria line. She had squeezed through the line and got right into Cheryl's face. "You'd better back off Cheryl Thomas, or else!"

Cheryl stepped backward, but then recovered, "Or else what?"

Margot had squinted, put her hands on her hips and said slowly, "Or else I'll kick your bucked-tooth face in."

Cheryl did have an overbite and was pretty touchy about it. I thought Cheryl was about to lunge at Margot, but the cafeteria lady yelled at us to move along or she'd call for a teacher. The rest of the year, Cheryl had made sure Margot wasn't around when she pushed or tripped me.

We rounded the corner of our street.

"I'll call you later," I said with little enthusiasm.

"Tomorrow will be great. High school is a whole new beginning." She gave me a slow motion punch in the arm. She walked down our street a few yards and turned, "Hey, if I see 3B or MGM, I'll ask if they've seen my bosom buddy lately." She giggled and kept walking.

I thought I was going to throw up.

Chapter 3

I peeked through the window in our kitchen door and saw Lisa's butt sticking out of the refrigerator. The cool air was glorious as I walked in.

"You're still eating?" I sat down at the kitchen table and adjusted the gauze away from the scrape.

"What?" She shut the door.

"You had your face in the fridge when I left."

"Oh." She laughed a little. "What happened?"

I sighed. "I fell off my bike. End of story."

"That looks bad."

"No, Mrs. Williamson just put lots of wrap on it. How was Sears?" *Please drop it.*

"We didn't go. Dad said he wasn't up for it."

"Really? Where is he? Where's Mom?"

"Upstairs. I think Mom's in the shower."

I limped upstairs and knocked on my parents' door. "Hello?"

"Alli?"

"Dad? Can I come in?"

"Sure, honey."

Dad was reading on his bed.

"How ya feeling?"

"Okay." He smiled and put the book down. "I just needed a little rest."

"Are we still going out?" I sat on the bed.

"Well, I don't want to disappoint those poor crabs. They're just dying for us to come." He chuckled.

"Good one." I sat on the fluffy comforter that Dad hated because it had flowers on it. I snuggled under his arm and raised my leg to show him the bandage.

"Oh, Lordy. Mom told me about your accident. How's it feeling?"

"Awful." I wasn't going to tell him the whole story.

"Well, it couldn't be as bad as being thrown into boiling water!" He tickled me with his hands pinching like claws, but it was only half-hearted.

"Alli?" Mom poked her head out of bathroom. "Honey? How's the leg?"

"It's okay."

"Let me see."

I glanced at Dad to make sure he watched me as I limped into the bathroom. "Look." I said to Mom and took off the bandage. The bathroom was steamy and smelled like Mom's Aveena shampoo that Lisa and I were not allowed to use— or even touch.

"Oooo. That's nasty. You poor baby." Mom wrapped her arms around me and rocked slightly back and forth. I melted like I was six again, hurt and afraid. Tears dribbled down my cheek and disappeared into the shoulder of her worn terrycloth robe.

"Mom, I can't face another year like last year."

She pulled away and looked me in the eyes. "Honey, I'm sure it won't be that bad."

"Mom, please." I wiped away any leftover weakness from my cheek and left. *She doesn't have a clue.*

I went into my bathroom to shower off the day. I scrubbed everywhere except the scrape; the shampoo soap stung it enough to count as cleaning. I dabbed it with a towel and took a good look at it. It was really just a bad scrape. The memory of Matt's face staring at my boob was a million zillion times more painful.

A few minutes later, Mom opened my bedroom door. "Alison, Dad still isn't one hundred percent. I called the Williamsons' and cancelled."

"What?" But we'd been planning it for days.

"I'm sorry. I know you were looking forward to going out tonight."

"Are you kidding?" Shock quickly turned to anger. "You're not serious."

"Alli, Dad isn't up for it." Her tone was irritated.

"He's just tired," I insisted.

Mom's eyes narrowed, warning me to shut up, but I really wanted to go out. I needed one fun thing to happen today, something to help me forget about tomorrow.

"So, we aren't going out because Dad is tired."

"You know what, missy?" She hissed the 's'.

"What?"

I guess she really didn't want me to ask.

"That's enough!" Her nostrils flared.

Oh jeez, she's got the nose thing going.

"You're not the only one having a bad day."

"Whatever," I mumbled.

She definitely didn't hear me because saying "whatever" sends her over the edge. She slammed the door shut.

I sat on my bed and stared at my leg. "Alison Collins, you are a spastic, boob-showing loser, and you are doomed tomorrow." I lay there, hating everything, especially my bubble gum pink curtains with big bow ties, hating the stupid pink comforter that was kind of scratchy, but never telling Mom because I begged her for it a couple of years ago.

Someone knocked on my door.

"Alli? Can I come in?" Dad cracked open the door.

"Hey, Dad. How ya feeling?" I knew I didn't sound sincere.

"Not too bad. How are you feeling?" He held something.

I shrugged. "What's that?"

"Well, it's something of Nana's." He sat down next to me.

"Really?"

"Mom and I were talking about how things are kind of tough for you right now."

"Oh." *Even Mom and Dad know I'm a loser.*

"This is Nana's journal." He looked down and rubbed the dark brown cover. "Honey, I know things have been hard since we've moved here. I don't know what it's like to be a fourteen-year-old girl." He smiled at me.

"It's not easy."

"It doesn't seem to be." He paused. "I wish I knew what to say to you to help you feel better."

"It's okay," I lied.

"I was lucky to have Nana. She always knew the right thing to say. I remembered this journal was in the attic. I don't know if it will help, but I thought you might like to have it."

"Thanks, Walt." I leaned over and kissed his stubbly cheek. "Wow, Nana's journal. I didn't know she had one."

"Well, she kept one off and on." He patted my knee and blinked a couple of times. He got up and walked to the door where he turned and looked at me. "My mother had a great gift. She always saw what was important. I see a lot of Nana in you."

"Thanks a lot, Dad." Once again, Dad made me feel better. I clutched the journal for a moment and looked up. "I love you."

He had already left.

I opened the leather cover, and a musty, powdery smell reminded me of her basement. I touched the yellowed pages, running my fingers over the words she wrote. A hot ache swelled in my chest as I raised the book to my face. *I miss you so much*. I leaned on my headboard and pulled my knees up so I still could still smell the Nana-ness as I opened the cover.

November 16

Michele and I are on our way!! Ten days with Dave in Morocco. I kissed Walt on the head as we left for the airport. He is so precious when he's sleeping. I don't know how I let Mom talk me into this. It's crazy!! Michele is so excited for this adventure; I guess I am too. It will be wonderful to see my brother after a year. I really don't know what to expect from this exotic place.

I read on; her voice echoed in my mind. She arrived in Morocco the next day and toured a Kasbah with her brother, soaking up all the different foods and traditions, and the colors and sounds of Rabat. Nana, Michele and Dad's Uncle Dave walked on stone paths, past carts pulled by donkeys, while run-down cars honked to clear the path. It sounded wild and scary. I remembered stories about Michele; Nana's best friend. They grew up together; Dad said they were actually distant cousins and went everywhere together.

November 20

I think it's about 7 in the morning, and I just woke to the sounds of bleating camels and men shouting in Arabic. Michele, Dave, Diane and I arrived here on the edge of the Sahara yesterday after a long, four-hour trip. Driving here was a terrifying game of chicken. Drivers seem to dare each other to swerve as they bomb toward each other on one lane roads! In addition, many of the roads were dirt,

*making for the bumpiest trip I have ever experienced.
I shut my eyes and said Hail Marys for about two
hours. Michele needed more than a nap, but that's
all any of us got when we finally arrived here on the
edge of a golden sea—the Sahara Desert. We are
staying at Maha's Oasis, which is touted as a hotel,
but I can assure you that it is very misleading. It's
like a permanent camp. I am literally lying in a tent
at this moment, and Dave and Diane are in the one
next door. We gathered in the main tent last night
and had dinner together. Our host or whatever,
Ramel, made us Pigeon Pie! Dave told us it is a
Moroccan specialty. We tried it, but filled up on the
veggies and cous cous. After dinner, we walked back
to our tents under the most beautiful night sky I have
ever seen. From horizon to horizon was a blanket of
dazzling lights! I swear there were more sparkling
stars than black sky last night. It was magical and
awe inspiring.*

*This morning we are off to ride camels! It's still
quite cold out, but the sun soon will be high and it
will warm up. I'm still a little sore from the bumpy
ride, but the adventure continues!!*

I was transported and energized by the story. I couldn't
believe Nana had never mentioned a trip to Morocco or the
desert. I got off my bed and grabbed my dictionary with a
world map in the back. My butt was numb from sitting so
long. I found Morocco at the top of Africa and located the

Sahara. So cool. Nana's trip sounded like an adventure from *Indiana Jones*. I lifted the worn pages to my chest, letting happiness radiated through me, but it evaporated when I realized the truth: *Nana rode camels in the Sahara, and I'm afraid of high school. Nice.*

September 1

Dearest Diary-a (get it??) di-a-ry-a!! Hee-he

I'm in the BEST mood today, so I'll write with my purple gel pen. OMG just when I thought the day was going to be boring, boring, boring the most hilarious thing I've ever seen happened. Spaz Collins fell off her kiddie-sized bike right in front of my house AND her boob fell out of her bathing suit top! It was the funniest thing I have EVER seen.

She takes loser to a whole new level. I was talking to Patti on the phone when I saw her sprawled on the road. Next thing I know, her boob's in my brother's face. She probably flashed him trying to impress him. I bet she saw one of those Girls Gone Wild Spring Break videos like the one Matt has under his bed and realized that is what you have to do to impress guys. She's such a freakin' loser. I can't wait to see her with Huge Snoz Margot tomorrow. Huge Snoz will probably be holding Alli's hand tomorrow defending her best spaz friend!! One can't go anywhere without the other one. They always walk right by my house in their stupid matching outfits.

WHAT LOSERS!!! (I had to change gel pens to red—my hate color)

Before Alli moved here, we used to hang out all the time. I really hate both of them!!!

I changed to blue because I went and got JB. It's

sad that JB is the only thing that calms me down. I just shoved it under my pillow, that's all. It calms me down just to know it's under my pillow and that's where I'll keep it. God help me if anyone ever finds out. I'm going to stop! I swear.

Chapter 4

Six thirty a.m. and my eyes were glued open because ping pong balls bounced in my stomach. *I have an hour to try and get myself decent.* I started downstairs, limping slightly from the scrape. Light streamed through the bottom of the door in the hall by the kitchen. *That's weird.* I knocked. "Hello?" No answer.

I opened the door. Dad was sleeping on the toilet; his body bent sideways and his head resting on the sink. *God!*

"Dad? Hey, Dad," I shook him a little and he didn't wake.

Something's wrong.

I ran upstairs to my parents' room. "Mom." My hand shook as I touched her shoulder.

She opened her eyes and squinted at me.

"Dad's asleep on the toilet downstairs." I swallowed hard.

"What did you say?"

"I can't wake Dad up." My voice cracked.

Mom sat up. She blinked and looked at the clock.

"What?" She seemed confused.

"I can't wake Dad up on the downstairs toilet."

"God almighty." She threw back the covers and ran downstairs.

"Mom. He's just asleep." I couldn't control the tremble in my voice. I followed her right into the bathroom.

"Walt! Walt!" She tried to shake him, but he didn't move.

"God. Oh God—Alli, help me." Her voice shook.

I grabbed his T-shirt—it was damp—and tried to move him, but his body slid away from me. It was so dense and heavy, like a huge bag of sand. He slumped onto the floor, his head hit the tile with a thud and his arm twisted under his body in an unnatural way. Cold terror rose in my gut.

"Dad." I grabbed his hand and tugged as hard as I could to pull him out of the bathroom but he barely moved.

"Stop, Alli!" Mom started to breathe into Dad's mouth and she pounded on his chest. "Walt! Please!" She put her fingers on his neck. "Dear God in heaven— please, Walt!"

This isn't real. This isn't real. I stepped away from Mom. My knees buckled, and I crouched into a ball, covering my face. *Please, make him wake up. Please, please.*

"What's wrong with Dad?" Lisa entered the bathroom doorway and looked at Mom and me with furrowed brows. "What happened?"

"I don't know. I don't know." *This is a nightmare. It's not real.*

"Call 911!" Mom screamed at me as she hovered over Dad.

"Alli! Do something!" Lisa eyes were wide with terror.

I ran to the phone—called 9-1-1—babbled answers to

the stupid questions the unsympathetic voice on the line asked. I gave our address and hung up. Mom was still desperately trying to give CPR.

"Mom, help's coming."

"How long?" She was white and her forehead glistened.

I felt cold—disconnected from my body.

"Alison!" Mom screamed.

"I don't know. They said they are on their way," I screamed back. *I'm so cold.* My heart pounded in my ears. *Where's help? Someone help us.* Every second crawled like a lifetime. Mrs. Williamson—the emergency course. I called Margot's number.

"Hello?" Bill answered.

"My dad—my dad's hurt. Please, help." I started to gasp. "My mom can't get him to wake up."

"Who is this?"

"Alli."

"Alli. Your dad's been hurt?"

"I don't know what's wrong. Help, please."

"Okay, have you called an ambulance?"

"Yes, but it's not here yet. We need someone now!" I started to sob.

"Okay, okay, honey. Try and stay calm. I'll send Elaine."

Lisa stood behind me crying. "Is someone going to help?"

"Mrs. Williamson's coming right now."

Mom held Dad's head, sobbing. "Don't leave me, Walt! Please," she begged. She laid her head on his chest. "Please, no." The morning sun shone through the sliding glass door and I could see the outline of her body through her nightgown as she bent over Dad.

I couldn't stay. I ran outside and the prickly brown grass hurt my feet. Something real. Mrs. Williamson was running up the street.

"Hurry, please. Hurry!" I ran toward her.

"Alli! Where's your dad?"

"On the kitchen floor."

"Is he conscious?"

"No."

We entered the kitchen and found Mom still pushing on Dad's chest and Lisa crying, crouched in the corner.

Mrs. Williamson rushed to Mom. "Janet, I'll take over. Does he have a pulse?"

"I don't know. I couldn't find one." Mom was ashen; her hair was matted on her face, wet from tears and sweat.

Mrs. Williamson put her fingers on Dad's neck, looked at us, but didn't say anything. She blew into his mouth and his chest rose, as the air left his chest a sputtering noise came out of his mouth. "One, two, three, four, five."

"Is he breathing?" I asked.

No answer.

I don't know how long it took, ten seconds—ten minutes, but the ambulance came and took Dad on a stretcher with Mom gripping his hand, crying. Mrs. Williamson followed the siren in our car, and within a few minutes other neighborhood women were in our kitchen cleaning and whispering. Mrs. Beckwith stirred something on the stove.

"Doctors can fix anything, right?" Lisa asked Mrs.

Beckwith as she put scrambled eggs in front of us. She hugged Lisa and said, "They'll try."

The smell of eggs nauseated me. *How long have they been gone?* I glanced at the clock, but couldn't remember what it said. I walked to the window and saw Margot, Cheryl and other kids waiting for the bus. Margot had on her new backpack and jeans. Margot and Cheryl were talking and looking at my house as the bus arrived. I went back into the kitchen. I was in a nightmare. *I want to wake up.*

Finally, Mrs. Williamson opened the kitchen door and guided Mom inside.

"There was nothing they could do," Mom whispered.

My mother's words clanged in my head like a trap door opening and I plummeted into blackness.

Chapter 5

Black spots danced in front of my eyes and my knees buckled. I ran to the bathroom and threw up. I gripped the toilet. Spinning, suffocating, blackness.

Mrs. Williamson knocked on the door. "Alli? Honey, let me in."

I flushed and laid my head on the seat cover trying to understand. "In a minute," I mumbled. I wanted to stay in that bathroom forever. He'd just been in here. I felt for a warm spot on the floor, like the imprint after you get out of bed. Nothing. Only cold.

I needed Mom.

I opened the door and saw her sitting at the kitchen table in her cotton nightgown. I stepped into the kitchen and Mrs. O'Connor's eyes met mine, but Mom gazed right through me. I ran and put my arms around her neck, but she didn't move. "Mom," I choked through tears.

She looked at me, stunned.

"Mom, it'll be okay." I grasped for anything to say.

She shook her head slowly, then reached up and clutched

me as if I were a life raft.

"Mom, please." *Tell me it's a horrible mistake.*

Mrs. O'Connor walked over and looked out the front window, shaking her head, wiping tears from her face.

Mom loosened her grip, got up, and splashed water on her face. When she looked at me it was as if she was a zombie—white, no expression, blood-shot eyes.

"What happened?" I asked.

"They said he had a heart attack. He was gone when we arrived at the hospital." She looked out the window for a minute and finally said, "Where's Lisa?"

"She's on the front lawn," Mrs. O'Connor answered. "Alli, why don't you go check on her?"

I obeyed, happy to leave the cold, lifeless kitchen. I open the kitchen door and like Alice falling into Wonderland, I was in another world—where sunshine and life existed. I sat on the burnt front lawn next to Lisa and looked around. The locusts were humming and people were still going on with life. How could the school buses run? How could happy kids still go to school? The world had left us behind; forgotten in the shadows. No one noticed that we weren't there.

"I want to go to school," Lisa said.

"Really?"

"I think so."

Mom had gone upstairs. Mrs. O'Connor said it was fine and made me walk Lisa over to the Huntsman Elementary principal's office. The secretary didn't look happy that we were late. School smelled of paper, meatloaf and pine cleaner—nothing had changed.

"Trouble getting up today, ladies?" she asked in an unpleasant way.

I said the only thing I could think of, "Our father died this morning." I didn't know how else to say this horrible fact that was now part of our life. The words just stumbled out.

"What a horrible thing to joke about!" She narrowed her eyes and glared. "What are your names?"

"This is my sister, Lisa Collins. She's in Mrs. Bealor's fifth grade class. I'm Alison Collins. I don't go here."

Lisa put her face in her hands, and I put my arm around her. "Are you sure you want to do this?"

The secretary's face went blank. "I'll call Mrs. Bealor."

Mrs. Bealor came out and said in a soothing voice, "Hi Lisa. I'm Mrs. Bealor. So, you want to give today a try?" Her voice quivered. "I know Mrs. Williamson; she called me a while ago." Tears were in her eyes. "I am so very sorry."

Lisa nodded, unable to speak. Mrs. Bealor wrapped her arms around her and gave her such a squeeze that Lisa's skirt hiked up a little and I could see her flowered underpants. She took Mrs. Bealor's hand, turned and waved goodbye.

The secretary looked down at her hands as I passed her on the way out.

****

Grandma and Pap Malone arrived from Pittsburgh by noon the next day. Grandma always arrived with foil-lined shoe boxes full of chocolate chip cookies. Not this time. Mom, Grandma and Pap talked a lot behind closed doors. A weird heaviness pervaded the house and made it hard to breathe. Lisa brought school work home with her, but she mainly watched TV from Pap's lap.

I kept expecting that Dad would walk through the door and I would wake from this nightmare. Nothing helped or relieved a vague pain pressing down on my chest. The door bell rang often with neighbors stopping by to deliver casseroles, fruit baskets and hushed words. Grandma and Pap answered the door. Mom stayed in her room.

Chapter 6

Fruit baskets, flowers, casseroles.
Silence.

Chapter 7

A black Army car drove us to church. Tons of adults I didn't know watched as an officer escorted my mother to the front pew. Lisa, Grandma, Pap and I followed. After we were seated an organ began "Amazing Grace" and heads turned to the back of the church. Eight officers carried the coffin in, gripping the rails with their white gloves. I felt weak, hollow and alone as I watched the coffin, draped in an American flag, glide slowly down the aisle.

Was Dad really in there? Dad! Stop, please. He was so close I could touch the coffin. *Stop! I'm sorry for whatever I did to make this happen. Please! This is a horrible mistake.*

A glance at Mom told me the truth. It's real. *Breathe, just breathe.*

Mom's face was chalk white, except for the dark shadows under her eyes. She looked used-up and frail in the black dress Grandma bought for her. I reached over and put my hand in hers. She didn't even flinch. Her fingers were cold, like she couldn't feel anything—like she was dead.

I slid my hand back into my lap and felt something crack

deep inside me. Raw grief seeped through me like a virus, killing every ounce of happiness I'd ever known. I tried to take a breath, but it was too hard; the black veil strangled me. I suffocated in grief.

Margot sat three rows behind me, and I kept hearing her sniff and blow her nose. I turned and looked at her. She mouthed something to me, but I couldn't make it out. I shook my head to signal I didn't understand. She cried harder and nuzzled her face into Bill's side. He put his arm around her and kissed her head. I watched through the murky darkness that separated me from everyone else. *Margot's got Bill. I've got—no one.*

The officers' practiced hands folded the flag and solemnly presented it to Mom. She buried her face in it and collapsed back into the pew. Pap clutched Mom under her arms, and we all followed the black coffin out of the church.

Chapter 8

"Mom?"

"What?" She looked at me as she made her bed. It had been four days since the funeral, and it was Lisa's tenth birthday. The dark circles under Mom's eyes punctuated her expressionless face.

"Can I help?"

"No, Alison." She sighed deeply. "Grandma and Pap are getting Lisa's cake and I…" She sat on the bed. "I don't think I'm going to be able to make it through this day."

"Are you okay?"

"Please, just leave me alone." Every word, every movement seemed to exhaust her. She looked at the needlepoint pillow she had made to decorate their bed and threw it weakly at the wall. "Alli, I don't think I can do this."

"Do what? Make the bed?" I knew better.

She looked up with tears dripping down her face. "No." She looked around and motioned to the room. "I can't do life." She wiped a drip from her nose. "I don't even want to get out of bed. All I want is Dad."

I sat down next to her and rubbed her back. "I'll finish, Mom. Go take a shower."

She got up without looking at me and wiped her face. "God, please give me strength," she whispered and walked into the bathroom.

Grandma and Pap bought a birthday cake that read, "Happy Birthday Lisa #10" on top. We never bought cakes; Mom always made them for us. The cake looked as fake sugary sweet as Grandma's enthusiasm, but I was glad because Mom couldn't even fake a smile for Lisa. Lisa said she was excited to get back to her friends, and I couldn't believe that my life was so bad that school didn't seem so horrible.

Something tightened in the pit of my stomach, as Grandma lit the candles. *Oh crap, singing.*

Dad had a habit of controlling every singing event by harmonizing loudly over everyone's voices, whether it was in the car, church or parties. He thought he was quite the Michael Buble.

We sang, but Mom wiped tears through the whole thing. I tried not to cry for Lisa's sake, but tears ran down my cheeks anyway. Lisa stared at the candles with her mouth turned slightly into a smile, but the flickering light in her eyes told the truth.

Grandma cut the cake and announced, "Lisa, I have something very special for you that I made myself." We expected something crocheted from Grandma on every gift-giving occasion. Last year, she crocheted little bells on everyone's Christmas presents. "You can also use them for

Christmas ornaments!" she informed us, thrilled to pieces.

We moved to the living room and Grandma handed Lisa her present. It was a store-bought sweater, but then she pulled out a matching crocheted hair band. Lisa darted a quick look at me and said, "Oh, Grandma. It's really nice. Thank you."

Grandma and Pap also gave her a pretty bracelet. It was a better present than she normally got. I was happy for her.

"You know I had to use my own allowance money for this," I said to Lisa as I handed her my gift.

"Thanks, Alli." She opened the frame decorated with hearts. "This is nice. I love it."

"Here you go, honey," Mom said in a soft voice as she handed Lisa a present.

Lisa ripped off the paper and squealed with delight.

"Oh, thanks, Mom. This is exactly what I wanted." It was a cell phone she'd begged for ever since I got one a year ago.

I got a cell phone when I was thirteen, Lisa gets one when she's ten. Whatever.

She started to pull the phone out of the box and Grandma said, "Lisa, you didn't open the card."

"Oh, yeah. Sorry." She opened the card and smiled as she read the front. Then her face contorted, horrified. She dropped the card and ran out of the room.

Mom covered her face and swore.

Grandma picked up the card and walked to her.

"We bought it together." Mom rubbed her face and looked up. "I don't know how to do this, Mom. It's too hard."

"No one knows how to do this, Janet." Grandma put the card on the table and wrapped her arms around Mom.

I grabbed the card and at the bottom it read, "Love Mom and Dad."

I knocked on Lisa's door with the phone in my hand. "Lisa, it's me." I opened the door and found her face buried in her pillow. She rolled over, her cheeks pink and tear-stained. "Do you think things will ever get better?"

I handed her the phone. "I don't know, Lis."

"I miss Dad so much," she cried.

"I do too." I put my arms around her. "We have each other."

"When Grandma and Pap leave tomorrow, do you think Mom will be okay?"

"I can't think about anything but getting through school tomorrow."

"I'm glad to go back," she said.

I smiled at her. "Hey."

"Yeah?"

"I love you. You can always count on me."

I took her phone from her and put my cell number in it and added the contact as Favorite Sister. "Here let's use the camera to take a picture to use as your screen saver." I pointed the camera at us and snapped. We looked at the picture and laughed at the horrible pink, swollen eyes on Lisa and my pathetic smile. "Two hot babes."

"I'll erase it," Lisa said.

"Don't you dare. I love it," I lied.

I went in my room and pulled the pillow over my head.

Dad, how could you leave me? How could you leave Lisa? Mom's completely lost without you. Nothing matters to her—nothing. I sobbed, gasping for breath, but it was so hard to breathe through the darkness. *How can I face high school without you?*

I sat up to take a deep breath and blow my nose, and a sick lurch in my stomach made me grab for the garbage can. I waited for a minute and the nausea turned to a dull dizziness. I slid off my bed and sat next to the garbage can. The edge of Nana's journal peeked out from under my bed. I'd forgotten all about it. I took a couple of deep breaths and opened it.

November 23

Sitting here on the back deck of Dave's house enjoying the warm and gorgeous weather with my best friend, Michele. She's the only one I know who would be up for this adventure! This morning, we were shocked to wake to a man chanting in Arabic at 5 a.m. over a loud speaker or something, far away. Dave explained that is to wake everyone up to pray. Muslims pray five times a day bowing toward Mecca or the East. Very, very different. I guess I shouldn't complain about 9 o'clock Sunday mass!

Dave's house has a cement wall that surrounds the whole tile house except for an iron gate in the front. Dave's maid is bringing us breakfast, and then we are going to travel to the Roman ruins at Volublis. Dave and Diane both can speak French fluently (thank God), and Dave has a few lines of Arabic down. (Praise Allah!)

Nana's handwriting calmed me. I sighed. Her journal sounded as if she was in the room talking to me.

November 27

While Michele is taking a bath (she says she smells like a donkey!), I have to write down the crazy experience we just had! We were in Fez, which was not in our plans, but Diane said she wanted to explore it as it was close to Volublis. Wow—this place was like stepping back into the Middle Ages! We were in the marketplace (called the Medina), which was a maze of high-walled, narrow alleys lined with street vendors. People, donkeys, sheep and carts crowded together through the narrow dirt alley. The overwhelming smell of animals, spices and food filled the air. Dave wandered away to buy olives, and I saw an old leathery skinned woman smile and wave me over. She was wedged between a man selling eggs and another selling leather slippers.

"Bon-jour," I greeted her.

She sat quietly for a moment, smiled and said, "Madame, I have something for you to buy." She spoke English.

"Really?" I was surprised because she was sitting behind an empty stall.

She pulled out a small black box and put her

47

hand on it. "This, Madame, is for you. It will help you and your daughter on life's journey."

She slid the box to me, and I opened it. It was an amethyst dragonfly ring. The top wings are lavender colored and the bottom wings are violet. It's so unique and striking; I'm wearing it right now.

Then, the weird part.

The old woman said, "The dragonfly is a symbol of two worlds, like you. You live in two worlds, the demands of raising a child by yourself and the demands of staying focused on your spirit. Right now, you are devoted to your child. But the ring will remind you that your spirit is waiting, and you will find your true sense of self with maturity."

I couldn't believe the woman knew about Walt!!!

"Actually, I have a son, not a daughter."

She smiled at me. "Yes. Try it on," she said in her thick accent.

It fit. She told me it was 20 Dirham—that was really a bargain.

Michele loved it. She asked if the woman had another one.

"No, Madame," she said with kindness in her voice. "The ring is meant for her. I can only sell things to people if they are meant to have them."

"I'm meant to have this ring?" I asked her.

"Yes. It will become part of your family's history."

"Well, what if I didn't want it?"

She smiled at me. "You did." There was something

*about her deep brown eyes that was kind and knowing.
I can't explain it.*

"Do you have anything for me?" Michele asked.

*"No, Madame. I am sorry. Insh'Allah." She
smiled again at us and pulled a black sheet across her
stall. I was still staring at the ring when we bumped
into Dave who had been looking for us. We told him
about the ring and walked back to the spot where she
was, but the stall was empty. Empty! Poof! It was the
craziest thing.*

I closed the journal and let my mind linger in Medina. I
could almost see the old woman and smell the spices. And
in wondering what happened to the ring, I forgot about
tomorrow, for a little while.

Chapter 9

Margot's face was framed by the kitchen window, and I raised my index finger giving her the "one second" signal. My sweaty palms made it hard to get a grip on my backpack zipper. *Calm down! You're going to school, not the gas chamber.* "Bye, Mom," I shouted. "I'm leaving."

No response. I pursed my lips and tried to ignore the gravy-thick silence.

Then Lisa called from upstairs, "Bye Alli. I hope you have a good day."

"Yeah. You too, Lis." It would have been nicer to hear it from Mom, but I'd take what I could get. "See ya." I hollered with saccharine enthusiasm and slipped though our door, hoping to keep the houses' gloom inside. The crystal clear air helped to clear my lungs, but heaviness still cloaked me.

"So? How was Lisa's birthday?" Margot asked.

"It was okay," I lied, shifting my backpack as if it were the cause of my discomfort. "Lisa got a cell phone."

"Really?" Margot's voice went up. "You had to wait until you were thirteen to get one."

"I don't care. I'm happy for her. That was the only good thing that happened. Remember how my dad used to sing?"

Margot laughed, but then realized what I meant. "Oh, man, that sucks."

I nodded. "Yeah, but last night I found something kinda cool." I didn't want Margot to know that I had been keeping the journal a secret from her. I looked at her, but she was staring ahead toward the bus stop.

"OMG," Margot said. "Do you see that smoke?"

We crossed the street to the bus stop, and I saw Cheryl Thomas pass a cigarette to Patty Kowalski, then tilt her head up and exhale a lungful of smoke.

"You're crazy," Margot said to Cheryl in what I thought was a very loud voice.

"Got a problem, Williamson?" Cheryl cocked her head slightly to the side.

Leave it be, Marg. Just leave it be. In an instant, the knot in my stomach and my pit stains doubled in size. Cheryl was a loose cannon, unpredictable and scary. Would she bring up the boob incident? *Don't look at her!*

"Let's wait for the bus over here," I slapped Margot on the arm and glared at her. "Stop it!" I hissed.

She ignored me. "If anyone sees you, Cheryl, your ass will be grass."

"Get a grip, loser," Patty said. Patty was fifteen, but looked like she was eighteen. She wore black eyeliner around her eyes, and I heard that she had already "done it" with a high school boy. Terrorment, with the emphasis on terror, is what I felt around those two.

"Can you believe that?" Margot wouldn't let it go.

"Leave them alone and stop staring!" I took a deep breath to calm down, but my breath was shaky. I saw the bus crest the hill and thought I might have a nervous breakdown right then and there before I even stepped foot on high school soil.

Cheryl grounded the cigarette out with her heel and slipped her backpack on.

"Well, what happened last night that was cool?" Margot asked.

"I'll tell you later." I darted a look at Cheryl. I couldn't think straight.

"Do you smell something?" Margot said loudly as the bus pitched forward.

Patty and Cheryl were two rows in front of us, and Patty turned and said, "You better shut your face, if you know what's good for you." Cheryl snickered.

"What are you trying to do?" I whispered. "God, Margot." *Couldn't she just let it go today? Just once for me?* I looked out the window and bit my lip trying to blink back the tears that constantly slipped down my cheeks no matter how hard I tried to stop them.

"See this?" She pointed to her back.

I flicked a tear and glanced at her.

"This is a back bone. You seriously need to get one."

Couldn't she see it? Didn't anyone notice how I sagged under the weight of this heaviness? I couldn't lift this suffocating grief that draped over me and distorted everything. Even the September leaves took on a grey cast as I stared out the window the rest of the way to school.

Margot and I lost each other in the swarm of kids that piled off the bus as we squeezed through the door. I remembered where my locker was from the orientation day in August, so I followed the flow of backpacks to the end of the hall counting down the locker numbers until I found mine. I unloaded my new notebooks and stuck a mirror on the inside of the door as the warning bell went off. My first period class, Consumer Science, was a few doors down from my locker and I easily found my way there before the last bell.

Mrs. Moore called roll. "Ginny Brooks?"

The girl next to me said, "Here."

"Alison Collins?"

"Here."

She looked at me with raised eyebrows. "Welcome, Alison. Did you enjoy your extra-long summer vacation?"

She might as well have slapped my face. "Yeah, I guess," I mumbled as heat rose up my face. The teacher was completely oblivious to the wound she'd just dealt me as she called the rest of the names.

"I'm really sorry about your dad," the girl named Ginny whispered to me. "Mrs. Moore is clueless."

"Thanks." I stared down at the table praying I could fight back tears. Mrs. Moore made us take notes on the horrors of salmonella and then gave us a demonstration on what I considered was a good way to get it. We gathered around her as she attempted separating egg yolks from their whites using only the shells. Ginny and I giggled as Mrs. Moore cracked an egg, tried to transfer the yolk into the shell, and *splat*.

"Hang on. This is how chefs do it." Her eyes were knit together in concentration as she cracked another egg, leaving the broken egg on the floor.

"Is she for real?" She reminded me of a *Saturday Night Live* skit where someone spoofs Martha Stewart or Julia Child.

"My mom just uses a do-hicky," someone suggested from the back of the crowd.

"Yes, but if you don't *have* a do-hicky, this is…dang it!" She spilled the yolk into the whites. She finally got one egg yolk to stay in the cracked shell. "There!" She beamed.

The bell rang.

"Ah, Alison, do you have a second?" she said wiping up egg goop from the floor. As others filed out she said, "I just wanted to apologize for before. I'm so sorry. I had no idea about your father." I guess someone had filled her in during class.

"It's okay." I couldn't think of anything else to say.

She shrugged her shoulders and pinched up her face, like she'd smelled something awful. "Well, at least he isn't suffering anymore."

Slap! I couldn't believe how stupid she was. I wanted to tell her, *He didn't suffer at all; he just dropped dead, leaving me alone in this world with grown-ups like you, Mom and the secretary at Lisa's school.* Instead, I bit my lip and for the third time that morning, trying to keep it together. *So far, so bad.*

Margot was waiting for me outside of English. "How's it going?"

"Don't ask."

Mrs. Nottingham, our English teacher, walked over to us.

"Are you Alison?"

"Yes."

"Welcome, honey." She put her hand on my shoulder. "We're going to start fresh today, okay? Anything you've missed in the past week will just be excused."

"Okay."

She had a very kind face and I could tell she knew.

"Can Alli sit next to me?" Margot asked. "I can help her get used to things."

"That's a great idea." She looked at the class. "Johnny, move to the front row, so Alison can sit next to Margot."

"What?" Johnny glared at us.

"That's the spirit," Mrs. Nottingham said winking at us, completely ignoring his irritation. "Would you like me to introduce you to the class?"

"No, thanks."

"Got it." She had pretty brown eyes that crinkled at the edges when she smiled. She gave my head a little rub, like she understood. My shoulders melted, and I took a deep breath for the first time today.

"Go ahead and sit down girls. Margot, I trust you to take care of Alison."

"She likes to be called Alli," Margot said.

"Okay. That's just what I'm talking about."

My breath felt almost normal as we made our way to the back of the room.

"She seems really cool," I said.

"Hello, all you bright bulbs," Mrs. Nottingham said loudly as the bell rang.

"She's seriously nuts," Margot said.

"What do you mean?" I whispered, but Mrs. Nottingham's voice interrupted us.

"Everyone take out your 'If I could change the world' essays and pass them up as I take roll."

"Well, like last week we were talking about the Holocaust, and she decided to read a few pages from *Number the Stars.*" Margot leaned in a little more, "She started to cry!" Margot took her finger and make the "crazy" loop around her temple. "She needs medical help."

I looked around the room as people passed up essays. Ginny Brooks looked at me and waved casually. I raised my eyebrows and nodded with a half smile.

Mrs. Nottingham gathered the essays. "I have the best possible news."

"You're leaving for a few weeks of recuperation?" Margot whispered to me.

"Any guesses?" she said with excitement in her voice.

"We get a study hall today?" someone called out.

"No. Much better. We are going to act out Scene II of *Romeo and Juliet.*"

A loud groan erupted.

"Come on, now. This is going to be fantastic! We're going to pick names out of the Volunteer bin for the different parts." She walked over to the other side of the room and wrote on a piece of paper, shoved it in a coffee tin, and came back to the front of the room.

Margot pinched her eyebrows together and mouthed *we?* and shook her head, looking disgusted. I thought it sounded kind of exciting.

"The part of Romeo goes to…" Mrs. Nottingham put her hand in the coffee tin labeled *Volunteer.* "Eric!"

Everyone looked over to a boy whose cheeks went scarlet. "Um, well, can I wait and see who Juliet is?" he asked. He seemed taller that the other boys, and had dark brown curly hair that dangled down his forehead, brushing along his eyelashes. His dark lashes framed crystal clear green eyes.

Jeez, he was really cute.

"Eric, you character!" Mrs. Nottingham laughed as if he were making a joke. "You'll be an exemplary Romeo!"

I hoped that was a good thing.

Mrs. Nottingham put her hand back in the bin. "Alison, I mean *Alli,* you have been volunteered to be Juliet! Isn't that wonderful?"

I felt the blood drain from my face.

Mrs. Nottingham looked at me with a thrilled smile. Now, I knew whose name she'd just thrown in the bin.

"Are you up for the challenge?"

Margot shook her head madly and mouthed, *no.*

"Yeah, okay."

"You will make a consummate Juliet!"

I smiled at Mrs. Nottingham. I had soup in a restaurant once that sounded like *consummate,* and I didn't like it. I looked over at Eric, and one side of his mouth turned up in a half smile. *Gulp.* I felt shaky but shrugged my shoulders and gave a little smile at him and looked back at Mrs. Nottingham. *Breathe,*

Breathe. I couldn't help taking another peek at Eric and bit the inside of my cheek so I wouldn't smile. *Romeo.*

"Ginny," was all I heard.

"Sure," Ginny's voice snapped me back to attention.

"What part did she get?" I whispered to Margot.

"The nurse. You're crazy to accept the part of Juliet."

"Do you know that Eric kid?" I tried to ask casually, but it didn't work because Margot slowly turned toward me with big eyes. It was shocking that she didn't want to be in the play because she had a real flair for dramatics.

"You're seriously crazy. Cheryl Thomas has liked Eric Prinz forever."

"Really?"

"Margot?" Mrs. Nottingham looked at us.

"Yes," Margot answered.

"Yes, you accept the role or yes with a question mark, indicating that you were not focused on me."

"Of course, it's yes I will accept the role."

"As…" Mrs. Nottingham was going make Margot suffer.

Oh, boy. I looked down at my hands, avoiding Mrs. Nottingham's disapproving eyes.

"As?"

"Peter, of course." Mrs. Nottingham smirked.

"Peter? A guy?"

"Yes, a guy. In Shakespeare's time, women weren't allowed to play any roles, so this is a kind of ironic justice wouldn't you say?"

"Oh, of course. That will be fun."

I snickered. Even though Mrs. Nottingham was killing

58

me with the big words, she was funny.

"Excellent." Mrs. Nottingham sighed and didn't look quite as enthusiastic as before.

"Hey, I want to tell you about last night," I whispered to Margot.

"What?" Margot hadn't heard me. "I can't memorize things. Did you see how she tricked me?"

"We can practice together. Listen, I found something of my grandmother's last night."

"Really? What?" Margot said.

"Nick, are you willing to be Friar Laurence?" Mrs. Nottingham looked over our way, narrowing her eyes. "There shouldn't be anyone talking but me."

Time to zip the lip. I didn't want Mrs. Nottingham to be mad at me.

She turned back. "Nick?"

"I thought you were the only one talking," Nick answered.

"Can you just answer the question, *please.*"

"Oh," he said. "Ah, what was the question?"

Mrs. Nottingham put both her hands on the desk and shouted, "Friar Laurence. Are you willing to play Friar Laurence?"

"Okay."

I don't think he had much of a choice.

Margot whispered to me, "What a loser. What did you find last night?"

Mrs. Nottingham looked at Margot. "Ms. Williamson, are you a friend or foe?"

"I don't know what a foe is."

"Opposite of friend. And I can assure you, you don't want to be a foe of mine."

Margot said, "Then, I guess friend."

Mrs. Nottingham smiled but in her eyes you could tell she wasn't happy at all. Her fakey-smile seemed dead on her lips. "Wise choice."

Tell you later I wrote on my notebook, and slid it to Margot.

Chapter 10

I struggled up the bus steps with what seemed like sixty pounds of books. Not all of my teachers wanted to make a "fresh start," and I had a ton of work to make-up. Margot waved to me from the seat in the middle of the bus. Cheryl was busy talking to some kid I didn't know, probably bullying money off him. I lugged my backpack onto the seat Margot held for me.

"What's up, Juliet?"

"Not much, Slave Boy Peter." I plopped down next to her.

"Hysterical. Now, what did you find last night?"

"A journal." I pushed the backpack on the floor. "My grandmother's."

"Oh. I was hoping it was diamonds or something."

"Well, it's kinda cool. She traveled to Morocco with her friend Michele when my dad was a baby. It's like her travel journal of their adventure and stuff."

"Did she meet some tall, dark stranger who rocked her world?"

"Why do you have to be so gross all the time? This is my nana you're talking about."

"My bad. Tell me about this adventure."

"Well, she met this gypsy-type woman that sold her a dragonfly ring."

"Gypsy woman? Seriously? Like with a nose ring?"

"I don't know." Margot was ruining it. Why did she have to make something I really liked sound dumb? "No rings in noses, just an amethyst dragonfly ring." I shouldn't have told her.

Margot's eyebrows rose, and her mouth turned down in a not-too-bad type of way.

"That's a brown stone, right?"

"No, it's purple. My birthstone."

"Have you seen this ring?"

"No. I don't know anything about it. I never even knew she traveled to Africa."

"Africa?"

"Yeah. That's where Morocco is. Up top and to the left."

"Really. I thought it was in France or something."

The bus's brakes squeaked loudly, and the door swung open at our stop.

"Do you want to come and see the journal?" We hopped off the bus, and I slid my arm through Margot's.

"Sure."

Cheryl yelled at us as she stepped off the bus, "Why don't you two kiss and get it over with? Time to come out of the closet, girls!"

"Go have a cigarette, Bucky!" Margot yelled then looked

at me and stuck out her front teeth and took a fake puff from a cigarette.

"Stop it!" I shook my head and laughed. "Bucky?"

"They can't all be gems, sister."

I didn't really know what to expect when we got to the kitchen door. Margot hadn't been to my house since after the funeral when everyone came over for sandwiches and coffee.

Why did people have a party when someone died? I expected to see Dad among the group of men in their dark green uniforms. I wanted to walk up to him and have him wrap his arm around my shoulder, pull me in tight, letting me know I was safe and everything would be all right. But he wasn't there, and things weren't all right.

I opened the kitchen door and saw dirty dishes in the sink. A moist, old-food smell filled the air.

"Mom?" No one answered. It felt like walking into a stranger's house. Everything looked the same; it just didn't *feel* the same. The air was thick and still. I glanced at Margot. She met my look with her eyebrows pinched. I hoped she might make a joke and lighten the atmosphere, but her jaw was clenched shut.

"I guess Mom went out. That's weird." Our car was in the driveway, but the house felt empty. We rounded the corner to go upstairs, and I noticed the curtains in the living room were drawn shut. More weirdness. Our house was always bright—windows wide open. I walked across the room to open the curtains.

"Leave them." Mom's voice made me jump as if she were a ghost.

"Mom?" I blinked several times and saw her sitting on the couch, still in her bathrobe, staring at the empty fireplace.

"Are you okay?" I saw Margot take a step backward, toward the kitchen. The only normal thing in my life was Margot, and I didn't want her to see Mom like this.

"Just leave me alone, Alli."

"You sure? Mom, let me open the windows." I wanted to make something seem normal.

Her eyes shifted from the fireplace to me. "Please. Leave me alone." Her whisper shook me like a scream. It was desperate and distant, nothing like my mother.

"Margot and I will be in my room." I passed Margot without looking at her and she silently followed me.

"How long has your mom been like this?" Margot asked once we were in my room.

My chest grew tight. What could I do? I wanted to protect Mom, but I wanted help too. "I haven't seen her like this before," I lied, shut the door and opened a window. I needed fresh air, and thankfully there was a breeze outside.

"Man, your house is really different." Margot's tone wasn't sympathetic, more accusatory.

"Yeah."

"Your room feels the same, though." She half smiled and sat on the bed.

"I spend a lot of time in here lately." I reached under my bed and pulled out the journal.

"Cool." Margot fanned the pages with her thumb. "Smells old."

"I swear I can almost smell my nana's perfume in the pages."

Margot put her nose to the journal. "Yeah, like dusty powder—kinda like my grandfather's basement." She handed me the journal and lay down on my bed. "Show me the part about the ring."

I flipped to the entry on November 27. "Here, read this page."

She put the journal directly in front of her face, and all I could see was her shiny, honey brown hair. She giggled, "Donkey." She peeked over the cover. "How do you say that Volub place?"

"I'm not sure."

She looked back down. "They speak French in Africa?"

"Apparently. Just keep reading." Over the next few minutes I watched the breeze blow through the golden streaks the summer had left in her hair. It must be nice to have beautiful, bouncy, golden streaks. Watching Margot relax in my room was more refreshing than the breeze.

She looked up and threw the journal on my bed. "This is seriously cool. You've never heard about this ring? Never saw it in her house?"

Don't throw that! "No, but my dad told me some of her stuff's in the attic. Be careful with that, Marg." I wasn't going to tell her how I got the journal. She might ruin my last memory of Dad. Obviously she didn't get how important this was to me; she just tossed Nana's journal like a candy wrapper. Those last few moments with him still warmed me, as if his words were lingering embers of a fire that had just gone out.

"You've got to find this ring."

"I have no idea if it's still around. I don't think it means anything. It's just a cool story." I eyed the journal on the bed. "I never saw her wear it. Besides, the gypsy woman told my nana that she had a daughter. The Collins family only had boys for a hundred years, until me." I walked over and picked it up carefully.

Margot watched me. "Holy frickin' guacamole."

"What?"

Margot jumped off the bed and started pacing. "You're the first granddaughter in a hundred years?"

"Yeah. I've told you that before."

She stopped in the middle of the room and pointed to me. "Daughter! You're the daughter! You are the daughter that the old...gimme that thing." She grabbed the journal out of my hands. "What did that woman say?" She flipped a few pages, "What was the date?"

"Be careful—I'll find it. Let me do it."

"Hold, on." She squinted at me, annoyed. "Take it easy, Alli. I've got it." She flipped the journal and ran her finger over the words. "Here. Right here. 'It will help you and your daughter on life's journey.' You're the first daughter that she had—her *grand* daughter."

An electrical current boomeranged through me and left my heart pounding with a tingly feeling in my fingers. *Is it possible? Didn't I read this right after I begged for a sign? Did Dad or Nana or whomever hear me? Is this the sign?*

"I've got goose bumps," Margot said. "This is incredible." She blinked a couple of times. "Alli!"

66

"What?"

"The ring is even your birthstone! This is unreal!" She grabbed me by the shoulders. "We've got to look for it."

Someone knocked on my door.

"Alli?" Lisa sounded frightened.

"Lisa?" I walked over and opened the door.

She was pale and her shoulders were pinched up as if she were cold.

"Lis, what's the matter?" I forgot everything when I saw her face.

"Have you seen Mom?" she asked.

"Is she still in the living room?"

"Yeah, crying in the dark. She wouldn't talk to me." Her voice softened into a whisper, "I'm scared, Alli."

Margot spoke up from behind me. "Listen Lisa, we're in the middle of something right now. Give us a minute." Did she have to sound so snotty and mean, as if she were talking to June?

I put my arm around Lisa's shoulder. "Don't talk to her like that."

"What's your problem, Alli?"

"What's *my* problem?" I couldn't believe she would ask me that. "She's scared, that's the problem. Life's a little scary these days, Margot." I yanked the journal out of her hands. "You haven't once asked me how I am since my dad died." My voice cracked and tears welled in my eyes. *Do not cry.* "My problem? *Our* problem is *we* can't pretend that nothing has happened. And then *my* problem is life doesn't go back to normal when I go home, or haven't you noticed?" Blood pulsed violently in my temples. "It's okay, Lisa. Margot's leaving."

Margot's mouth gaped open, but just for a second. She clamped it shut and narrowed her eyes. She took a deep breath and threw her shoulders back and walked to the door. "Alli, this house and everyone in it is *seriously* whacked. *Everyone*—" She glared at Lisa. "—is losing it." She looked back at me and said slowly, "I'll see you around." The problem with nerves of steel is that you can't *feel* anything.

I bit my lip and looked away. One blink and she would see the tears, so I stared out the window. She passed Lisa who stood frozen in the doorway.

"Don't worry about it, Lisa. She didn't mean it." I knew I didn't sound convincing.

"She's right," Lisa whispered. "This house isn't home anymore. Nothing is the same."

If I opened my mouth I would fall apart. Lisa wrapped her thin little arms around me. The afternoon sun had dipped, and we held each other in the darkened hall between our rooms. I felt like we were alone on an island.

Stranded.

Chapter 11

Happiness was a distant memory. Could Dad and Nana really be trying to help me? Impossible. I'd never felt so alone.

"Hey, we'll be okay." I let go of Lisa, and dug deep until I found my numb place, where I could act like I was in a dream.

"Mom's really freaking me out, Alli."

"How was Mrs. Bealor's class today?" I needed to talk about something there were answers to. Like school.

"Pretty good. Things were kinda normal. She gave me a hug as I was leaving today."

"Do you have any homework?"

"Yeah, math. I have to learn my multiplication tables up to nine."

"Well, get started, and let me know if you need help. I'm going to check on Mom."

"I want something to eat."

"I'll bring it up." Lisa didn't need to see Mom again.

I peeked around the corner into the living room. The

floral couch was empty. I pulled the curtains back and sighed. The darkness wasn't natural. It was a beautiful September day out there. Something more than a wall separated us from the world, and I was getting sick of it. The sun filtered through the trees and brightened the living room. It looked Williamsburg Blue again, not like a morgue. Don't ask me how the very same Prairie Blue chairs from Kansas changed to Williamsburg Blue when we moved to Virginia. Mom joked that it was all in the sun's angle. Jeez— Mom joking. That seemed like a million years ago. I couldn't remember how long it had been since she had smiled.

I wandered into the kitchen and found her leaning over the sink. Hoping to steal some affection, I slid my arms around her waist and nuzzled my face into her terry cloth robe. She glanced around with a vacant expression—a discarded rag doll. Her face was almost grey, her nose and eyes were pink, and her hair matted to her head. After a silent moment, she lifted a soapy hand out of the water and put it around my shoulder.

Mom, please love me. I breathed in the familiar soft terry cloth robe that had been a part of Mom for as long as I could remember.

She turned and wrapped her other hand around me and I clung to her from the deepest, darkest space in my soul where my sadness, fear and loneliness lived. Slowly, Mom's rigid body softened around me, and I squeezed tighter. She pulled away. "Alli, I don't know how to get through the days."

"I know," was as all I could say although I wanted to say, *please hurry up and figure out a way because Lisa is terrified and I don't know how to be a mother to both her and you.* "Go take a bath, and you'll feel better."

I heard her bedroom door close as I poured Lisa a glass of milk—the last of it—and got her the last two chocolate chip cookies. I put the milk and cookies next to Lisa's worksheet on her desk.

"Thanks, Alli. Did Mom come upstairs?"

"Yeah, she said she thought she'd feel better if she took a shower." I fake smiled from my numb place.

Lisa smiled back and dunked her cookie in the milk.

I kissed her on the cheek. "Things will be okay. I promise."

She nodded while she chewed. Her pigtails bounced like gold coils.

"I'll be downstairs." I took each stair slowly thinking about Margot's comments. *Losing it.* Screw her. I could kill her for saying that in front of Lisa. If Mom couldn't protect her, I would.

Washing the dishes was a relief. It was something I could do to help make the house seem normal. "Mom?" I yelled from the bottom of the stairs. "How about if I make breakfast for dinner?"

"Yeah!" I heard Lisa answer from her room.

"Okay." I thought I heard from Mom.

Breakfast for dinner was always a treat for us. Mom used to whip up pancakes and bacon, and Lisa and I would pour syrup over everything. It was the greatest. I opened the fridge—I forgot—no milk. Well, pancakes were out; I rummaged around. No bacon either. I found eggs. I guess fried eggs counted as breakfast. We had bread for toast and jelly. I cracked an egg over the frying pan and separated the yolk from the white as I dropped it in the pan. *No problem, Mrs. Moore.* I could take care of things at home after all. I did the yolk thing better than Mrs. Moore, and the mother thing better than Mom.

"Breakfast is ready!" I yelled. Lisa came down the stairs smiling and Mom followed—hair brushed and a pair of grey sweatpants and T-shirt.

Lisa sat at the table. "Can I have some milk?"

"We're out," I said. "We need groceries, Mom."

"Okay," Mom said. "I'll go out tomorrow." She looked down at her plate, uncertain and afraid, like a child getting on a bike for the first time.

I ignored her expression, we needed food. "Thanks, Mom." I winked at Lisa, but she didn't see me. She was looking at Mom.

After our egg dinner was cleaned up, I sat on the side of my bed, exhausted. My first day of school was over, thank God. School wasn't the worst thing in my life—home was. The journal still lay on the bed, and the afternoon rushed back. Margot—the daughter connection—the fight. I put my head on my pillow and opened up the journal again.

The dragonfly is a symbol of two worlds, like you....It will help you and your daughter on life's journey...you are meant to have it. It will become part of your family's history.

I moved my fingers across the words and let them sink

72

in. *Was it a sign? Was I the daughter? Is Dad or Nana trying to help me from the other side?* My heart pounded against my ribs. I put the journal on my face and wished I could melt into the pages. A message for me? A shred of hope found in a dragonfly ring.

I shot up. *Wait, a dragonfly.* White shock pierced me. *Like the one at Nana's funeral!* A glimmer of light tore through the dark veil. Warm hope. I pulled my knees up to my face in a tight little ball. *Don't do it, Alli. It will only hurt again. Go to the numb place.*

Tears filled with warm, squishey, gooey hope streamed down my face. *Please, PLEASE be true.*

The ring. I had to find the ring. If I found it, I'd know it was true. That was the only way to know for sure. Could I sneak into the attic now? No, Mom would hear. It was too late. I got under my covers and clutched the journal. *Tomorrow. I'll look tomorrow.*

"Alli?" Lisa's voice woke me.

"Hhmm."

"Alli."

"What's wrong?"

Lisa stood over me in her underpants with her hands clutched around her waist shivering. "I wet the bed." Her voice was wobbly and she wiped a tear from her cheek.

"Oh, Lis. It's okay." I couldn't remember the last time she wet the bed. "Take off your wet pants and get in my bed. I'll get you some dry clothes."

"Are you going to tell Mom?"

"No. I'll take care of it."

I staggered into her bedroom that was cast in shadows by the bathroom nightlight, and could smell pee right away. I could see well enough to pull the sheets off her bed and get to her dresser.

"Here you go." I handed Lisa fresh underpants and a T-shirt, then grabbed the wet undies. I threw everything down the laundry chute in the hall. I hoped the *swoosh* wouldn't wake Mom.

I walked back in my room and stepped on the journal. It must have fallen on the floor when I tossed the covers back. Hope fluttered again.

"Scooch over," I said, signaling that she could sleep with me.

"Thank you so much, Alli." There was relief in her voice.

I slid under the warm covers, and Lisa snuggled up behind me. I winced when I felt the warm dampness from Lisa's legs on mine, but didn't have the heart to tell her how gross it was.

September 15

Dear Diary,

I'm writing in brown today because I feel like crap. Nothing good is happening in high school. Everyone hangs all over Matt. I am as invisible at school as I am at home. At least in junior high, you're king of the hill. All the kids were scared of you and respected you—but not in high school.

Matt, Matt, Matt is all I hear all the time. "Hey, are you Matt Thomas' little sister?" Girls flock to me when they find out. Of course they say we don't look anything alike. Shocker! He has perfectly white straight teeth (no matter how many times he gets mangled on the field—GGGRRRR) and mine stick out further every day.

People are going crazy about him everywhere we go because he scored the game winner last Friday night during the home opener. For God's sake, you'd think he won *The Bachelor* or something. I'll be even less than a zero now. If I walked in the kitchen naked, Dad would say, "Cheryl, go upstairs...You're blocking my view of Matt!"

Well, at least I can do whatever I want and no one will notice. I have a pack of Marlboro Lights in my sock drawer right now! It will be just like the time Mom and Dad forgot about me and locked me out of the house. They completely forgot that I was supposed to be grounded for stealing barrettes and just left me hanging outside when they went off to one of Matt's games. Eric told me they had no idea where I was until he asked about me at the game. He is the one person I can count on. Sure, Matt and Travis are best buds, but Eric and I are BFFs. (Hopefully SOON with benefits.) I'm sure we'll go to prom together and then get married.

I want to stand at the top of the stairs and scream, "Hey I'm alive too!" Instead, I grab JB and pull my sheets over my head and cry.

Chapter 12

Margot's face didn't appear in the kitchen window the next morning. *Shocker.* She held a grudge like it was her job. Of course, Mom was nowhere to be seen or heard. "I'm leaving," I yelled for Lisa's sake. *Liar.*

The bus pulled up to the stop as I got to the corner.

"Wait!" I ran across the street. "Thanks," I said breathlessly to the driver, who smiled as she shut the door.

The seat next to Margot, my seat, was open, but as I walked toward her she put her back pack on the seat and looked out the window. Cheryl Thomas and Patti Kowalski were in the back row watching.

"Can I sit here?" I asked Margot.

She didn't say anything, so I moved the backpack and sat. We bobbed in unison as the bus made its way to school. I didn't know what to say; I wasn't sorry, but I hated fighting.

"Say, Alli. Did you meet any *boobs* yet?" Cheryl said loud enough for the whole back of the bus to hear.

Oh my God. I felt heat rise up my neck and glanced at

Margot, who cracked a big evil smile. I bit my lip and looked down. Cheryl knew. God help me.

"Be careful, Alli. You never know when some boob will jump out at you and ruin your day," Cheryl said. Patti laughed hysterically.

I turned and looked at Cheryl, that freakin' witch. She clutched her hands over her boobs and made a horrified face.

Everyone in the back was in on the joke now, and the laughter shot into me like hot daggers. This was actually happening—worse than my naked nightmares. I couldn't run away. Hot, hollow loneliness, too thick for light or air, clamped down on me—and only me.

Margot's shoulders shook with laughter as she looked out the bus window. I got up and moved closer to the front of the bus. Thankfully, I could see school. I ran off the bus as soon as it stopped, staggered to the bathroom, and locked the stall. "Just breathe— numb place—it's okay." I sat on the toilet seat and put my head in between my knees. *Deep breaths. Think about Nana, the ring. I'll look for it tonight. Deep breaths. Clear your thoughts. Numb. Numb.* It was working. I opened my eyes and focused on a message on the wall. "Renee is a slute." I pulled a pen out of my backpack, crossed out *Renee* and wrote *Cheryl,* then scratched out the E on *slute,* so it was spelled correctly—*slut.* First bell rang. Four minutes to get to Consumer Science.

Ginny Brooks' smiling face greeted me and helped erase the horrible reality that waited for me beyond these doors. My breath settled into a regular rhythm as Mrs. Moore started class.

"I am going to make brownies today and demonstrate how to measure ingredients. If you have a recipe that calls for a quarter cup of water, how much would that be in a fraction?"

"One-fourth cup," someone yelled from the side of the room.

"Yes, excellent." She poured water into a measuring cup.

"Now, if your recipe calls for one half cup of oil, you could combine the liquid ingredients together. How could we measure this?" She gave a ridiculous confused face, like she was talking to first graders. Ginny looked at me and rolled her eyes. She seemed really nice. I could hang with her instead of Margot in English. Mrs. Moore called on another girl.

"Well, you already have one-fourth, and a half is two fourths, so you would fill the cup to three-fourths to combine the ingredients."

"Yes, that's exactly right. Isn't that a clever trick?" She smiled like she was talking to first graders and letting us in on some great secret.

"Whooooops," she said, her eyes opened wide. "Well, ah, that wasn't supposed to happen." She chuckled to herself.

Jeez. She should be a pre-school teacher.

"That proves that you have to be very careful when you pour."

Ginny and I looked at each other and laughed.

"Hmmmm, well, this is...oh, I know." She pulled out a turkey baster from a drawer and held it up for us to see. "This should do it, right?" She squeezed the bulb and stuck it into the liquid.

Ginny passed me a note as Mrs. Moore continued to work the baster.

All she needs is a red ball on her nose.

I enjoyed the rest of the period picturing Mrs. Moore in a clown costume.

The bell rang just as Bozo—I mean Mrs. Moore—put the brownies in the oven.

"You want to walk to English, Juliet?" Ginny asked.

Ka-ching! "Yeah, sure, Nurse."

The desks were all pushed to the sides of the room when we entered English. One side of the room had a blue banner that said *Montague* and on the opposite side of the room was a red banner, *Capulet*.

"This is cool," Ginny said.

Other kids came in and we all stood in the middle of the class. Mrs. Nottingham wasn't there yet.

"What's going on?" Johnny said as he came in.

"I guess we're starting the play today," I said.

"Welcome, my thespians." Mrs. Nottingham entered from stage left with a basket full of red, white and blue T-shirts.

Margot entered right behind Mrs. Nottingham and stopped dead in her tracks. "What did you call us?" I thought Margot's tone was disrespectful.

"Thespians, Margot. I know you'll be an excellent one. Does anyone know the meaning of this word?"

We stared at her from the middle of the room.

"Thomeone who liketh girths?" a chubby boy said.

Everyone giggled but Margot.

"A thespian is an Ac-*tor, Charles,*" Mrs. Nottingham said and dropped the basket. As if on cue, she struck a pose, framed her hands around her face, bulged her eyes, and made an "O" with her mouth. She looked like a mime who just got kicked in the butt.

"Oh my God," Margot said from the middle of the group.

I wanted to smack her for being so rude.

"Okay, here we go. All the Capulets take a red T-shirt and go over there." Mrs. Nottingham motioned toward the red banner.

"I don't know which house I am," Nick said.

"Go with the Capulets for today, Nicholas." She threw him a white T-shirt. "If you didn't get a part, or if you're Friar Laurence—" She smiled at Nick, "—take a white T-shirt and just pick a side."

The huge red T-shirt looked like a dress on me.

"Okay, here are some markers. Put your name on the front shoulder, and put your character's name or your stage job on the front and back of the t-shirt. These will be your costumes."

"Are these all extra large?" Ginny's T-shirt was big enough for a family to fit in.

"Do you know what a feud is?" Mrs. Nottingham asked the class.

I raised my hand. "A fight or an argument?"

"That's right Alli. A fight between families." I looked over at Margot.

"The Montagues and Capulets were two families who hated each other. Cousins, aunts and uncles of both families hated each other. These two families lived in Verona, Italy." She pointed to the chalkboard, where "VERONA" was written. "Okay, so on this side of the room are the Capulets. You guys hate the Montagues. What would you say to them in today's language to insult them if you met them on the street?"

"Seriously?" Margot said.

"Much of Shakespeare's language is based on insults and puns. It's hard for us to understand because we don't use these words to insult anymore. So, I wanted us to understand the unrest in Verona between the two families by insulting each other in today's language."

"Oh, boy," Nick said.

Margot stared right at me "You mean like a crazy, zit-faced bit—"

"In school-appropriate language." Mrs. Nottingham interrupted. "I want you to brainstorm as a family and then we will have a grudge match."

"Cool," Nick said. "I'll write."

Everyone started talking at once. "Scum, creeper, loser, dog breath, chum, greasy pig, fat, dumb ass."

He laughed as he wrote, but stopped. "You can't say ass."

Charles said, "It's in the Bible."

"Ah Mrs. Nottingham, can we use—"

"Would you say it in front of your mother?" she called over the noise before Nick finished.

"No." He shook his head at Charles as he answered.

I glanced over at the Montagues and caught Eric looking over at me. I smiled quickly and tried to act casual, like I was trying to see something over his shoulder. *Ahhhhhh!* I wondered if he could see my pink cheeks all the way across the room.

"Okay, let's get the insults organized," Mrs. Nottingham said.

"Pick several people to represent your family, and they will hurl an insult. Once it is launched, I will use Shakespearean language to match that insult. So, I want each family to write down four insults, and then you will stand up here and say, 'You, blankety, blankety, blank.'"

She walked over to the board and wrote:

Insult: You __adj__ (description), __adj-adj__ (description), __noun__ (thing).

"Are you watching, kids? This fragment needs to be grammatically correct." She looked at us. "You know what I mean."

Blank stares.

"Here's an example. *You nasty, bad-breathed donkey.*"

"See?" Mrs. Nottingham looked for a response from our group, so I nodded.

She smiled at me, but the Montague side was talking, so she glared at them, "Do. You. Un. Der. Stand?" She banged the chalk on the board with each syllable.

"Yes," Eric said to Mrs. Nottingham. He was so cute and polite.

"I definitely want to be one of the hurlers," Margot said in her typical nerves-of-steel tone and glanced at me.

Don't look at me, you 3B. We were both Capulets, what could she do? *Get real, what wouldn't she do?* My stomach clenched into a knot, and the thought of Margot combined with the potential of having to stand up and say something awful in front of Eric reminded me of one of Nana's favorite sayings. "Now, that situation, dahlin', would put me right ov-a the edge." *Yep. Right ova the edge.*

"I want to do one," Charles said.

"Me too," Nick said.

"I'll go," a girl with red hair said.

Hallelujah. I won't have to go.

"Huddle up," Nick said. "I don't want the *Monta-gooz* hearing."

A little terrorment bubbled around in my stomach when I looked at Margot, so I peeked over Charles' head and stared at the back of Eric's wavy brown hair. *Reminds me of brown velvet.*

"Okay let's get this going. Montagues, you go first. Once you throw your insult, wait for me to translate it into Shakespearean language."

A girl came forward first and stood in front of the rest of the Montagues.

She looked at her paper and shifted on her feet. "Ah, you smelly, butt-kissing zero."

The Montagues cheered. She sighed and cracked a little smile. Her neck was covered in pink blotchy spots.

"Okay, very good, Kara. Now let me think…How about, 'Thou churlish, rump-fed dogfish.'" I laughed and caught Eric looking my way with a smile that turned his eyes into half moons. A thrill shot down to my toes.

"Now—the Capulets' turn."

Nick walked out in front of us, laughing. "You, Montagues," he pointed at them and raised his voice, "You idiotic, toilet-licking warts."

We all yelled and clapped. Nick shook his hands over his head in victory. Even Margot laughed.

"Good job, Nick. And Capulets. Okay Shakespeare might say, 'Thou sottish, onion-eyed clotpole.'"

Nick looked smug and pointed at the blue team. "Clotpoles!"

"Montagues? Who's up?" Mrs. Nottingham said.

Johnny walked up and looked at each of us with one hand on his hip, looked down at his paper and read, "You moronic, booger-eating slut." He looked at the paper again and said, "I mean sluts."

The Montagues whooped.

Mrs. Nottingham smiled and nodded her head with approval, then rubbed her chin thoughtfully. "Let me see. How about, 'Thou knavish, ill-bred wench.'" She raised her voice, "Let's keep this G-rated, folks, okay? Last one—we only have a couple of minutes. Capulets?"

Margot got up and looked at me. "I'll go."

What's her deal? I took a deep breath and felt a throb in my stomach.

She faced the Montagues. "You absolute foul, zit-sucking ass."

"Margot," Mrs. Nottingham's voice went down an octave. "That's really unacceptable. I am sorry you chose to push it and ruin it for everyone."

"Seriously, they can say slut, but I can't say ass?"

85

Charles mumbled, "It's in the Bible."

Mrs. Nottingham's eyebrows pinched, she crossed her arms and locked her eyes on Margot. "I *just* told everyone to keep it G-rated."

"I meant it like, donkey."

What a complete 3B, would she ever shut up?

"I think we'll call home after school, Miss Williamson, and see what your mother thinks."

Margot sat down and looked at me with narrow eyes and I felt her hate rays.

What did I do?

"Everyone, start reviewing your lines. We're going to start reading tomorrow."

The bell rang.

"Margot, I want to see you before you leave."

"That was intense," Ginny said to me as we walked out.

"Her mom will freak when Mrs. Nottingham calls home." *Serves her right.* I was glad she was in trouble. She clearly didn't have my back. *Anymore.*

Chapter 13

Margot wasn't on the bus on the way home. It felt good to stretch my legs across the seat; my lower back ached, probably from all the heavy books. Cheryl seemed unusually pleasant and chatty to Patti Kowlaski. I was happy to slouch down, become invisible, and not think about Cheryl or Margot. I hoped Mom remembered to go to the store; I didn't want to look into an empty fridge again.

Five boxes of taco shells and peanut butter littered the kitchen table when I walked in the side door. A couple of grocery bags slumped on the counter and Mom sat on a chair with the phone gripped in her hand.

"Uh–huh, well. I'm not sure, really." She glanced up and looked more withered than yesterday.

I listened as I put the groceries away.

"Well, I'll talk to her. Thanks for calling. I'm sure we can get her back on track."

Quiet.

I put hamburger in the fridge.

"I appreciate that. Thank you again, Mrs. Bealor. Goodbye." She hung up the phone and sat on the kitchen chair.

"What's up, Mom?"

"Lisa's really behind in school."

"What did Mrs. Bealor say?"

"That Lisa missed lots of work the week she was out and now seems lost and overwhelmed in class. I guess she found lots of unfinished worksheets jammed in the back of her desk today." Mom leaned over and rubbed her face with her hands. "I don't know what to do."

I opened a bag of cookies. "Mom, did you buy milk?"

Nothing. She'd brought home five boxes of taco shells, but no milk.

"Mom, we need milk." I looked in the refrigerator. "And eggs."

"I don't know what to do about Lisa."

"Mom, could you just go to Quick Mart and get some milk and eggs?" I took a breath, "What we need is milk and eggs, not a life supply of taco shells."

Mom grabbed the keys. "They were on sale," she snapped and walked out.

I stood at the sliding glass door and stared out into the back deck. Only a few weeks ago I'd watched Dad polish his boots there. Life was perfect then, and I didn't know it. Shoe polish and sweat. *Dad, I miss you so much.* I bit my trembling lip so I wouldn't crumble into a sobbing mess. *Why did you leave me?*

The ring.

I ran upstairs and pulled the cord to the attic stairs. Hot and musty air met me as I stepped onto the planks of the makeshift floor. I'd never been past the first couple of stairs–only far enough to help Dad bring down the holiday boxes. I carefully walked past the Christmas stuff and saw Dad's handwriting on three boxes: *Mom's stuff.* I opened one box but it only held Nana's ceramic Christmas tree with the glow lights and other ornaments that I vaguely recognized. Not in here.

The second box held scarves, gloves and small jewelry boxes. My heart raced. *Is it possible?* My hands shook as I opened one of the small boxes. Pins, brooches and clip-on earrings. *I knew it was too good to be true.* In the next small container was a string of pearls that Nana used to wear all the time. This was my memory of her—pearls and clip-on earrings, not a dragonfly ring. It was laced with the odor of Nana's perfume and a sad smile tugged at the corner of my mouth. *Alison, you're a fool to believe in anything other than this.* I stuck my face in and inhaled the precious memories. Gloucester, her laughter, the beach. The memories flooded my soul with her love.

That tingly electric feeling hit me again. Perfume. Nana's journal smelled like this. Maybe Dad had pulled the journal from this box. I pulled out all the scarves and gloves and found more small boxes at the bottom. I opened a white square box—a bracelet. Then, in the shadows, I saw a black ring box. I held my breath and felt my heart pound in my fingertips, too terrified to touch it. Hope in a black box. I licked my lips, reached in. *Please God, please Nana, please Dad—let this be true.*

I slowly opened the box and there it was. The dragonfly ring.

Tarnished and smaller than I imagined, but a treasure none-the-less. An amethyst dragonfly ring. I took it out and put it on. It fit. Warmth flooded me. *Someone loves me. I do count.* Hot, squishy tears filled with gratitude streamed down my cheeks.

"Alli?"

I jumped.

"Lis?" I hurried and put everything back but the ring and black box and wiped my face on my shirt.

"Hey, Alli, what are you doing?" Lisa stood at the bottom of the stairs.

I climbed down the stairs backwards. "I was looking through Nana's boxes."

"Really? Why?"

"Just a strange urge. Look what I found." I showed Lisa the ring on my finger.

"That's cool, I guess." She raised her eyebrows.

"It will be prettier when I polish it."

Lisa shrugged. "Where's Mom?"

"She ran to Quick Mart. She'll be home in a minute." I took a deep breath. "Hey, Mrs. Bealor called Mom."

"Really?" She immediately looked nervous.

"How's school going?"

"Well, it's hard. I never know what's going on, but I really, really like Mrs. Bealor."

"Yeah, well I guess she found all your unfinished papers in the back of your desk."

"Oh, no." Lisa covered her mouth, "Is Mom going to take me out of Mrs. Bealor's class? But Mrs. Bealor put her

arm around me today and said I was doing a good job."
Lisa's little face flushed pink trying to stop the tears that were
teetering in her eyes.

"I know Mrs. Bealor is really nice. Don't worry, I bet we
can work this out. How about we do your homework
together every night until you get caught up?"

"Really?" Lisa looked at me. "You'd do that for me?" She
blinked and let the tears leak down her cheeks. "Do you
think I'll get to stay in my class?"

"Lisa, no one has said anything about taking you out of
Mrs. Bealor's class."

"Well, I just thought because I was confused all the time,
I'd have to go to a special class or something."

I heard the kitchen door shut. "Let's talk to Mom."

Mom's head was in the refrigerator as we entered the
kitchen.

"Hey Mom," Lisa greeted her.

She turned around, "Oh, Lisa." She looked at Lisa and
then me expectantly.

"Mom, Lisa and I were wondering if you thought it was
a good idea if I helped Lisa with her homework every night
after dinner."

"Oh?" She had one hand on the refrigerator and blinked
thoughtfully. After a second she cocked her head and half-
smiled. "That sounds like a good idea."

"How about I make tacos for dinner?" I said.

"I'll grate the cheese for you," Lisa said.

"Thanks, girls." Mom sighed. "I'll be in my room."

I reached in the fridge and the ring seemed to glimmer

magically at me. My heart skipped a beat. Anything was possible. Then I realized the ring was reflecting off the dome light in the cheese drawer. I didn't care.

"Here's the cheese." I winked at Lisa. "Get grating."

After dinner, Lisa and I set up in the dining room.

"Get some pencils and my sharpener from my back pack. Grab all your homework papers."

"We can do our homework together from now on." Lisa smiled at me.

She seemed determined to rip her math homework with her eraser. She erased every answer, redid the problem, and erased again to make it neater. The whole paper turned into a smear of gray. *Well, she finished, and we didn't have to get out the scotch tape.*

"Okay. Good job, Lis. Let's put the math homework in your red math folder and pack it all away in your backpack for the morning."

Lisa concentrated on her backpack and I wiggled my ring finger, letting the light catch the crystals.

After we finished, I went straight for the cabinet in the kitchen with the silver polish and locked myself in my room. I polished that ring until the silver gleamed. I slipped it on and watched the amethysts sparkle. How had Nana described the stones? I grabbed the journal and flipped to the right entry.

> *She pulled out a small black box and put her hand on it. "This, Madame, is for you. It will help you and your daughter on life's journey."*
>
> *She slid the box to me and I opened it. It was an*

amethyst dragonfly ring. The top wings are lavender colored and the bottom wings are violet. It's so unique and striking; I'm wearing it right now!

I looked at the ring sparkling on my finger and smiled. A miracle.

The old woman said, "The dragonfly is a symbol of two worlds, like you. The ring will remind you that your spirit is waiting and you will find your true sense of self with maturity." I can only sell things to people if they are meant to have them."

"I'm meant to have this ring?" I asked her.

"Yes, it will become part of your family's history."

"Well, what if I didn't want it?"

"You did." She smiled. There was something about her deep brown eyes that was kind. I can't explain it.

Unbelievable. Two worlds. And in one of them my spirits waited for *me*. I sat there, clutching the journal, and wearing the ring. *Nana, Dad, God—thank you.*

September 16

Dearest Diary (hey, if you switch the I and A in diary, you get dairy!! Mooooooooooo.)

I guess you can tell I'm in a great mood! The purple gel pen doesn't lie! Life is great, high school is great, and my friend Margot is great! That's right—Margot finally wised up about how much of a loser Alli Collins is and wants to hang out. I don't think I've mentioned it yet, but Alli's dad died on the first day of school. It was really weird, and it's all anyone on the street has talked about for a couple of weeks. Anyhow, I guess Alli's house is totally weird and Alli has shown herself to be a total loser and Margot has wised up and came running back.

Last night Margot came over and we watched *The Amityville Horror*. It totally freaked me out! Margot said that it reminded her of Alli's house...all haunted and crap with Col. Collins's ghost. After the freaky movie, I knew I couldn't last the whole night without JB. I don't know how I'm ever gonna stop. I just can't do it!!

Chapter 14

The next morning, I opened my eyes and half convinced myself it had to be a dream, but my hand peeked out from under the sheets and there it was, still sparkling. As my feet hit the floor, I realized my backache was still there. Worse, I hadn't had time to review my Juliet lines last night because getting Lisa and her homework fixed had filled my mind. A nervous flutter interrupted my backache and the crampy feeling in my stomach as I thought about Eric's emerald green eyes looking at me. *Am I getting period cramps?*

I brushed my teeth and looked under the sink for some pads and found an empty Maxi-pad bag. Great, another thing Mom had forgotten, but the sparkling dragonfly flashed on my hand and reminded me someone was watching over me. I smiled and walked into Lisa's room. "Are you okay for school today?"

"Yeah, I think so." She smiled and stretched in bed. "Thanks again."

My good mood got the better of me and I walked over and kissed her. "Good luck today."

Habit caused me to look out the kitchen window even though I knew Margot wouldn't be there. I missed my friend, like I missed everything from before. The grass completely covered my ankles as I stepped on our front lawn. The yard was Dad's domain; he had spent hours tending to the grass and garden. No one had touched it since Pap mowed it after the funeral and crabgrass and weeds infiltrated the border. One more job for me. I looked across the street. Terrorment. Margot and Cheryl were chatting nose to nose at the bus stop. I felt like a rabbit walking into a den of wolves. Margot hated Cheryl; they didn't have anything in common. Except hating me. They stepped away from each other as soon as they saw me cross the street. I kept my distance and stared at my feet, praying for the bus to come.

"Hey, Travis," Cheryl yelled.

I looked up and saw a Mustang pull up to the curb in front of Margot and Cheryl. MGM lounged in the passenger seat. *Dear God in heaven help me! Just run home! No, look away. No, run!* Heat rose up my neck and my feet glued themselves to the ground. I hadn't seen MGM since the boob/ bike disaster. My stomach seized into one tight knot. I tried to calm the pounding in my chest and breathed slowly through my nose.

"Hey, can I have a ride?" Cheryl leaned into the driver's side of the Mustang.

"Not today. We have a couple of other guys to pick up," the Travis guy said without ever looking at her.

I watched out of the corner of my eye. Travis had brown

wavy hair and a square jaw. Very handsome. Cheryl looked like a hooker from the movies as she twirled her hair and stuck one hip out. She leaned on the car's open window frame.

"Come on," she whined. "How come Eric gets a ride, but you won't take me?"

I blinked and stared at the ground. Eric was in the car? My hands shook so I shoved them in my pockets and felt my heart beat in my fingertips.

"Cheryl," Matt yelled, "Get back."

I glanced over to see her pout and step back. I thought the car would pull away, but it didn't. It rolled forward and stopped in front of me.

Help.

"Hey, Alli," Matt said in a velvety sweet voice.

Against my will, I looked at him. This could be very, very bad. I glanced in the back seat at Eric. I thought I might throw-up; my stomach was churning so much.

"I just wanted you to know how sorry I was to hear about your dad." His dark brown eyes peeked out from his bangs. Was it possible he'd gotten better looking?

"Oh, ah, thanks." Could anyone see my heart pounding through my T-shirt? Everyone at the bus stop stared at me. I felt wetness in my pits and pinched my arms closer to my body.

"Eric tells me you're in his English class."

There wasn't any spit in my mouth. "Uh huh."

"Alli's Juliet and I'm Romeo in our class play. Today's the first day of practice." Eric leaned over from the back seat.

97

Matt looked at me and smiled. "Cool." He fake punched Travis on the shoulder and said, "Your little bro as Romeo. Apple doesn't fall far from the tree, eh?"

What's that supposed to mean? I gulped but nothing was there to swallow. I smacked my lips to drum up something. No luck.

"Well, we gotta get going." Matt raised his hand in a casual wave.

"See ya." I looked at the ground as they pulled away. *This didn't just happen.* I knew everyone was staring at me, but I couldn't move. I forced the edges of my mouth down to fight the smile that crept up. My God Matt Thomas, Travis and Eric Prinz just stopped and talked to me! And they were nice! The ring. It had to be the ring.

The bus pulled up, and I got to the end of the line and took the seat closest to the front. I leaned my head against the seat and relived the miracle that just happened.

"You better keep your distance from him." A voice hissed in my ear.

I turned to see Cheryl squeezed onto the edge of the seat behind me, pressing against the two kids that were already there. Up close, I could really see that her overbite had gotten worse. An image of Cheryl chomping on a carrot saying "Gwoovy baby" flashed through my mind.

"Me and Eric have been together for years. Our families vacation together."

"I didn't do anything." I couldn't look at her. The image of a bugsy Austin Powers might make me laugh, and then I'd be dead meat.

"Margot told me you've been asking about him and flirting with him in class."

"No, I haven't." My voice sounded calm.

"You'll be sorry, you slut, if you throw yourself at him again. First, you flash my brother, now you throw yourself at my boyfriend."

"What?"

"Margot told me."

I snapped. I turned around and squared my shoulders to hers. "Margot told you what?" I glared back at Margot. "That Eric smiled at me? Or that falling off my bike and practically killing myself was a well planned event?" When I yelled a little spit flew in Cheryl's face.

The bus driver looked in the rear view mirror and noticed Cheryl hanging off a seat.

"Hey, get back to your seat," she yelled over the bus engine.

Cheryl wiped her face. "Oh, no you didn't." She shoved my shoulder and teetered back to her seat. I didn't mean to spit in her face, it was an accident. *Crap.* I shook from nerves, but this time it was different. It felt good to stand up for myself. I looked down to find the ring curled inside my clenched fist.

Chapter 15

I bounded off the bus and oozed through the crowds all the way to my locker. After a few deep breaths, I stooped down to the bookshelf and tried to figure out what I needed for the day.

"Alli?"

I turned to find Eric Prinz looming over me.

Holy frijoles!—Get up and say something intelligent. I steadied myself on the locker as I stood up with an arm full of books. "Hey."

He leaned on one leg, and then shifted to the other. "I, uh, well. I just wanted to tell you that, you know, I'm sorry my brother didn't give you a ride to school."

"Oh." His eyes were making it impossible to think straight.

"No, really. We would have, but Travis promised two other guys rides."

"Me? Why would you give me a ride? I thought you and Cheryl—you know. You would have given Cheryl a ride, right?"

"What?" Eric screwed up his mouth like something

tasted horrible. "Cheryl Thomas? I can't stand her."

"Really? I thought your families hung out together and stuff."

"Our parents are friends, but I can't help that. I always get stuck hanging out with her. It's seriously torture."

"Oh—I thought—she said—" *Stop talking!*

"She said what?" He narrowed his eyes, and he stepped a little closer.

"Oh never mind." *She'll rip my head off if she finds out I blabbed to Eric.* I grabbed my locker door and shut it. My sweater caught on the metal hinge of the lock and pinned me to the locker. "Oh, no." I wanted to die—*you're such a spaz*—as Eric watched me fight the locker.

"Oh, man." His eyes bulged as he put his hand over his mouth.

"Oh, it's okay. I'm fine. Really, you'll be late to class." I didn't know what to do. Drop my books? Yank my good sweater with all my might? The familiar burn of embarrassment ran through my blood.

"Here, let me help. Give me your books." He smiled and his warm, soft hand brushed mine. Every hair on my arm stood on end, and my stomach felt like it pinged down to my toes and ponged back up my throat.

Eric's cheeks flushed a light crimson.

I turned to my locker, shaking like a leaf and fumbled with the dial. Thankfully, I heard the *click* and freed myself. "Thanks for holding my books."

"Sure. No problem, Alli."

His said my name so sweetly, I winced. In that instance,

only for a heartbeat, I thought maybe he was looking at me and could see everything, even the heavy veil of sadness that covered me, as if his kindness peeked under the darkness and let in a ray of light. My bottom lip trembled, so I busied myself reshaping the pulled threads of my sweater.

"How 'bout if I walk you to class? You know, since I have your books."

I looked at his emerald green eyes and I swear I thought my heart popped. Add a sprinkle of freckles that covered his nose, brown bangs that dusted long dark lashes and I couldn't feel my arms or legs.

"No, thanks. My class is right there. I'm fine." I didn't want him to see the tears in my eyes.

He nodded. "Okay. Well, I'll see ya in English, Juliet." A couple of dimples punctuated his smile and it took my breath away. Then turned and disappeared into a crowd of kids.

A spasm of raw happiness rippled through me. *What just happened?* Did that beautiful boy just see me like no one else had been able to? I put my hand on the locker and took a deep breath and the dragonfly sparkled on my finger. The ring! The ring is *my* bling! A hip hop beat popped into my head and joy ricocheted around me. I felt like pumping my hands in the air and strutting. *Oh yeah, O yeah. You like this thing? My ringy thing? This ring wit wings? Jump back, hold on tight, dis sista's got it right. This ring. This ring's got some special bling.* The tune floated around in my head and I couldn't help bobbing my head a little as I floated into Consumer Science. I slid into my seat still feeling warm and wonderful. "Hi," I whispered to Ginny.

She looked at me with a suspicious smile. "What's up?" she mouthed.

I shifted in my seat and rubbed my hands together, desperate to tell someone Eric Prinz had just talked to me, but *something* felt strange downstairs. I shifted in my seat again, and yes there was a definite wetness down there. Not good.

"Ginny Brooks?" Mrs. Moore took roll.

"Here."

"Alison Collins?" Mrs. Moore called.

"Here. Ah, may I please run to the bathroom?"

She nodded and kept reading roll.

I hustled to the bathroom, each step confirming that *something bad* was going on. I locked the stall and discovered a big dark ruby spot in the crotch of my jeans. *God, so much blood. What am I going to do?* I dabbed as much of the blood out of my pants and underpants as I could. Even though I was used to getting my period, I couldn't get used to how gross and bloody it was. I bunched up a wad of toilet paper and tried to make a temporary pad, but needed a minute to figure out what I was going to do. I blew my nose and sat there, stuck. I wanted to go home. I wanted Mom.

I got a new wad, shoved it in place, took off my sweater, even though I only had on a tank-top under it, tied it around my waist and snuck through the halls. If anyone caught a glimpse of the blood stain, it would be worse than the boob incident. Well, maybe not worse, but definitely in the same ballpark. I crept like a secret agent, checking around corners and tip-toeing through the halls all the way to the nurse's office. There, a boy sat in a waiting chair in the nurse's office with an ice pack over one eye.

Crap. Now what?

The nurse's badge read, Nurse Taylor.

"Yes?" Nurse Taylor's voice was very pleasant, like that first whiff of chocolate chip cookies baking.

"Um, I don't feel well."

"Let's go in the back, shall we?" She pointed to the back room.

I side-stepped by the boy, so nervous he might catch a peek of blood that I practically jumped across the room.

She shut the door. "What's the matter, honey?" It felt like someone opened the steam valve on my pressure cooker situation. I let out a horrible combination gasp/cry that sounded like a dying cat.

"Are you bleeding?" I nodded, pinching my lips shut so I wouldn't let out another ghastly noise, and a tear trickled down my cheek.

"Period?"

"Yes." I whispered. "I bled all the way through my pants."

"Oh, dear." She rubbed my back, and handed me a tissue. "Is this your first period?

"No."

"Listen, this happens all the time. There are supplies in the bathroom to clean up and pads and things. Do you need some help?"

"No, I think I'll be okay." I took a deep breath, calming slightly as I walked into the rest room. "Do you think you could call my mom to come and get me?"

"Of course, honey. What's your name?"

"Alison Collins."

"I'll call while you're in the bathroom."

"You won't say anything in front of that boy, will you?"

"No, of course not." She smiled and rubbed my back again.

"Thanks" I cleaned myself up as best I could, re-tied my sweater around my waist and walked out of the bathroom. Ice-pack boy was still there.

Nurse Taylor winked at me and said, "Your mom's on her way. Have a seat."

"I didn't tell my teacher that I was coming here."

"Who is your first period teacher?"

"Mrs. Moore."

"I'll call her and let her know you are leaving."

"Thank you for all your help." I couldn't help but feel like a pathetic loser. I'd never heard of anyone bleeding all over themselves before. I sat next to ice pack boy watching the clock. He left after a few minutes; I kept watching the second hand move—tick, tick, tick. *She should be here in a couple of minutes, maybe ten or fifteen if she takes a shower. Shower? Ha—okay, so in, say five minutes, she should be here..* Tick. Tick. Tick.

No Mom.

"Do you want me to give your Mom another call?" Nurse Taylor popped out of the back room after fifteen minutes, looking surprised to still see me.

"Um, no, thanks." *Could this get any worse?*

She walked back into her office and I stood up to see if

the blood had seeped through my sweater onto the seat.

Mom entered the nurse's office forty-five minutes later wearing a sweat-shirt, and she clearly had not brushed her hair. "Let's go."

Silently, I followed her to the car.

Chapter 16

"Period, huh?" she asked flatly as we pulled out of the school lot.

I stared out the window. "Yep." *Couldn't she be nice for a second? Maybe have a little sympathy like Nurse Taylor?*

"Well, you're not the only one who's having a bad morning."

"Thanks for coming so quickly." I shifted miserably in my seat. I didn't care what kind of bad day Mom was having, because every day was bad for her. I got blood all over my pants, and I'm sure everyone in school knew now since Cheryl saw me coming out of the nurse's office. "You know, Sylvia Perez's mom took her to get a manicure when she got her period."

"Well, this isn't your first period, and to be honest, Alli, I don't think getting your period needs to be treated like a fatal disease. It's just part of life."

Houses zipped by as we drove and I thought that every other house must be happier than ours. "Mom, I think something special has happened to me."

Mom sighed. "I don't think menstruating is special."

"I'm not talking about my period."

"What are you talking about?" Her voice was accusing.

"Well." I took a deep breath. "I found something of Nana Collins'." I looked at her to make sure she was listening.

"Yeah?"

"It's a ring. A dragonfly ring." I flashed it at her.

"Where'd you find that?"

"In the attic. In Nana's stuff." *Now I'm going to get in trouble for going in the attic without asking.*

"And?" She sounded annoyed. I hardly recognized Mom anymore. Sunken eyes and a permanent frown completed her miserable expression. Of course she didn't care I climbed into the attic without asking. She didn't care about anything.

"Well, I think I am supposed to have this ring, because of something I read in Nana's journal. You know the one Dad gave me…" I couldn't say *the last day he was alive,* so I mumbled, "On Labor Day."

She blinked. "Yes. I remember."

"Well, the journal is from a trip Nana took to Morocco when Dad was a baby." Mom nodded but didn't look away from the road. "One entry is when Nana met an old woman, like a gypsy or something, and who sold her this ring." I pointed to my finger. "The old woman said the dragonfly represents two worlds, and it was meant for her *and her daughter* to remind them that, well, people from beyond are always watching out for you."

"What?" Mom didn't sound impressed.

Okay, maybe that hadn't come out right.

"I think I am supposed to have this. It's like a message from Dad or Nana to let me know that they are watching out for me, for us."

Mom shook her head. "Alli, stop it."

"Mom, I'm serious."

"Alison, please don't do this to me. We're on our own. The end. If that ring makes you feel better, well, I'm glad, but I don't think anyone is looking out for us."

"Mom, if you would read the journal—"

"Stop it," she yelled. "I don't want to hear any more about this." We pulled into our driveway, and she yanked the keys out of the ignition. "And don't you fill Lisa's head with this nonsense, either."

"Do I have to go back to school today?" I felt like crap.

"I don't care."

Of course you don't.

Chapter 17

Add menstruation to the list of no friends, a dead dad and a useless mother to sum up the joys in my life. I lay on my bed and lifted my hand so that the sun's rays sparkled on the one bright spot. The golden light made my finger see-through pink. I wiggled my translucent finger, and the wings seemed to flutter and dance on my hand. To tell you the truth, I didn't care if the ring was secretly meant for me or not; it was a part of Nana's past and now it was a part of me. I grabbed the journal and put it under my pillow where the musty powder smell soothed me. I bathed in the comforting scent and the warmth of the sun.

A door slammed downstairs. Groggy, I rubbed my eyes and noticed the sun had dipped creating bars of light and dark throughout my room. The clock read three in the afternoon! Aching cramps brought me back to reality as I stretched and got up. I felt like a zombie rising from the dead as I staggered downstairs and heard crying. Lisa's crying.

"Hey, Lis, what's up?" I rubbed my eyes again.

"Nothing." She wiped her nose and looked at me. "Were you sleeping?"

"Uh, yeah. Did something happen at school?"

"No, nothing happened at school. Are you sick or something?" She sniffed.

"Kind of. So, you're not crying about school?"

Lisa shook her head. "No. School was good. Mrs. Bealor said she was proud of me today. She put her arm around me and said I did great on my homework." Her weak smile disappeared when she looked at me. "What's wrong with you? You look like you're sick."

"Oh. I got my period and had terrible cramps. I feel better now." *White lie.*

"Oh." She wiped her watery eyes.

"I'm proud of you, Lisa." I rubbed her back. "You'll be caught up in no time."

"Alli?"

"Yeah?"

"I'm glad you're my sister. You make me feel like how it used to be, you know, before."

I was glad someone appreciated me. "So, what's with the tears?"

"I hate the Williamsons."

"The Williamsons? Why?"

"June Williamson came up to me on the way home from school and wanted to know if I was scared to live in a haunted house."

"What?" My chest tightened.

"June said she knew why Mom had gone crazy. It's because Dad haunts us all night."

"Are you kidding? Why would she say something dumb

like that?"

"Margot told her."

I gritted my teeth and felt rage pulsing through my veins.

Lisa sat at the kitchen table and rested her chin in her hands. "I told June that Dad's not haunting us and even if he was, I'd be glad to see him and—and Mom's just really sad." Her voice cracked. "I don't like people talking about Mom." Tears streamed over her freckles.

"Scooch over." The two of us still fit on one kitchen chair. "Lisa, I think that Dad is watching us, but like an angel, you know, not in a scary way. I feel like he's protecting and loving us from heaven. It helps me to think of him that way." I rubbed the back of her head. "We both know Mom's not crazy. You're right that Mom's sad. Very sad."

"I'm not sure anymore." Lisa stared at her hands.

My heartbeat pounded in my ears. Anger seemed to be my new best friend, and I was going to use it on my old one. I'd had enough. "Why don't you make yourself a peanut butter sandwich and watch a little T.V.? I'll take care of the Williamsons."

"Lisa?" Mom called from the top of the stairs.

"Hey, Mom." Lisa strained to sound normal and she reached for the peanut butter in the cupboard.

"Is Alli down there?"

"Yeah. I'm here."

"I want to talk to you two." She walked into the kitchen still looking like she did when she picked me up from school— sweats and matted hair. "I've been on the phone with Grandma and Pap." She leaned on the kitchen counter.

"They think we should move back to Connellsville."

"What?" Mom's words hit me like a punch in the stomach. "Are you kidding? You hate it there." Moving to Pennsylvania would not help anything. Old houses covered in grimy soot from the good ole days when folks worked at the steel mill. Now, all the mills had closed, and jobless people sat out on their run-down front porches watching the grass grow. Visits to Connellsville were always depressing. Everyone and everything smelled like left-over mill smog and cigarettes—disgusting. The opposite of the wonderful smells of the ocean and Nana's house.

"Well, my family would be close by. They're worried about us." She swallowed. "I'm worried about us."

"Well, I am not moving. It's horrible and depressing there. You don't even like to visit," I said.

"I don't know, girls. I don't know if I can make it on my own. Grandma and Pap would help out."

"Help out? How? Take Lisa and me to the Dairy Queen and see the drug deals? I suppose that means I would go to Marshall Middle School?"

"God, I know."

"Didn't Grandma mention that they've put a metal detector in the schools now? Maybe I'd get lucky enough to be shanked before Algebra," I couldn't help myself—but Mom didn't even look startled.

"I don't want to leave here. I like my school." Tears started down Lisa's face again.

I caught a glimpse of the dragonfly ring and remembered I had more strength than I knew. "Mom do *you* want to move back to Connellsville?" I didn't wait for an answer. "It's gross! The smoke from the mills still covers the town. It should be called White-Trashville. And you think moving there is going to solve our problems?"

Mom looked out the kitchen window and sighed. "I don't know." Then she turned and a hint of a smile crept up on her face. "Alison Anne, you are becoming a woman."

"What's that mean?" Lisa asked.

"People say when you get your period, you've become a woman." I shifted uncomfortably where I stood.

"Ugh. That's gross." Lisa shot a horrified glance at my crotch.

In a silver moment, Mom's face softened and she laughed.

In that second, the air changed like the first fragrant scent of a spring flower, but it didn't last. Mom's shoulders shook from laughter, and then, as if her body rejected happiness, her face contorted and she broke into sobs. She grabbed the counter and braced herself. "Oh, God help me."

"Mom?" Lisa looked confused.

"Moving home would be the death of me." She tightened her fingers on the tile counter. "I don't know how we are going to manage financially, but moving back to that God-forsaken town isn't the answer." Mom wiped her face with her dirty sweat shirt. She nodded to the peanut butter jar that Lisa held. "I'm glad you like peanut butter, Lisa. We may have to survive on peanut butter and hot dogs for a while."

"I'll eat peanut butter with hot dogs everyday if we can stay here."

Mom broke into a crooked smile.

I moved toward the door. "I'm going to go to the Williamson's to get homework from Margot."

Lisa's smile faded. For once, I was glad that Mom didn't notice anything.

Chapter 18

With every step I seethed about Margot and her rotten personality. Nerves of steel, my butt. Heart of steel was more like it. How could she ever have been my best friend? Now, she's hanging out with Cheryl Thomas? Those two witches deserved each other. I could take anyone's crap, but don't ever, *ever* mess with my sister. *Poor June. Margot would never defend her. Matter of fact, she makes that poor kid's life torture.*

I knocked on the screen door, and the scent of chicken, or stew or whatever delicious meal Mrs. Williamson cooked wafted from the kitchen. June's face appeared on the other side of the mesh.

"Hey, June. Is Margot around?"

"Hi, Alli." She smiled sweetly and yelled, "Margot, Alli's here."

In the distance I heard, "Are you kidding?"

June looked baffled. "No, I'm not kidding."

Mrs. Williamson walked in the kitchen and stirred the bubbling pot of yum. "Alli, honey. Come in."

She put down the wooden spoon and opened her arms

motioning me to come for a hug. "Honey, how are you?" She rocked me in her maternal warmth, then pulled back and looked me straight in the eyes.

"Okay." My voice cracked. *How did Margot get so mean when she has such a great mom?*

"How's your mom?"

"Okay, I guess." I stepped away from her. It was really hard to lie to her.

"You call if you need anything."

"Thanks." What a joke. What would I do, call and say "Hi, Mrs. Williamson. Could you help me remove the knife in my back that your daughter stabbed me with?"

"What's up?" Margot walked into the kitchen with her arms crossed.

"Hey, I was wondering what I missed in English."

"Let's go outside." She chilled the whole room as she walked past me and pushed open the screen door.

"Bye, Mrs. Williamson."

"Call if you need anything, honey."

"Thank you." I followed Margot out onto the driveway.

Margot smirked. "You missed it today."

"Oh?"

"Since you weren't there, I got to be Juliet." I bit the inside of my cheek and looked at my feet—casual like. "You know, once you get close, Eric has seriously gorgeous eyes."

Think of the ring. "I'm sure Cheryl would love to hear that from you."

Margot narrowed her eyes. "You've changed. Not for the better."

"What is your problem?"

"You're my problem," she yelled.

"What have I done?"

"Your whole family has gone crazy."

Her words were like a hot poker searing my chest and stoking the anger. "What? You told June that my house was haunted!"

She laughed. "I wanted to scare her."

"You told June that my mom was crazy!"

"Give me a break, Alli. Your mom has seriously lost it."

I lunged at her. I was going to tear her face off. "I could kill you," I screamed and yanked her hair with all my strength. She was going to pay for everything that had ruined my life.

She reached up and an icy pain shot through me as her nails ripped into my arm. "You're a freak show. You're all losers!"

"If you ever, *ever* talk about my sister or my mom again, I'll murder you!"

"Girls!" Mrs. Williamson yelled as the kitchen door slammed behind her. "What is going on?"

I let go of Margot's hair. We stepped apart panting.

She grabbed Margot by the arm and glared at me. "What's the meaning of this?"

I couldn't put words to my pain. Everything, everyone was horrible. My life was a disaster, and I couldn't change anything.

"She started it." Margot rubbed her head.

"What is going on?" Mrs. Williamson looked at us sternly.

Neither of us looked at her or said anything. The weight of her disappointment crushed me and my lip quivered.

After a moment of deafening silence, she said, "Alli, you should go home."

I clenched my jaw to try and stop the tears, but the combination of Margot's claws and Mrs. Williamson's words tore me in two.

I walked home with my head and arm throbbing. Mom was on the phone when I walked in.

"Yes, here she is, Elaine." Of course Mrs. Williamson had called. "Uh-huh, that would be lovely. That's fine."

I walked past Mom, straight into the bathroom and shut the door. I stuck my arm under cold water and gritted my teeth as I lathered. God, it looked like a tiger got a hold of me; I hoped I'd left a bleeding, bald spot on Margot's head.

"Alli?" Mom called from the other side of the door.

"I'm fine, Mom." I didn't want to talk.

"Alli, is this about what June said to Lisa?"

I turned off the water. Lisa had probably blabbed as soon as I got to the end of the driveway.

"It's not just that."

"Open the door, Alison."

I blotted my scratches with toilet paper, and the ring gleamed in the light as I opened the door.

"What happened?" There was more accusation than concern in her voice. Figured. "Is there anything I can do?"

"Anything you can do?" I laughed.

Mom looked confused. "Yes, I want to help."

"Well, I've got an idea. Show up."

"What?"

"Show up for me. Show up for Lisa!" Rage shot back to the surface.

Mom took one step back and leaned on the wall. "Alison, I know it's been hard for you two, but you can't imagine how hard it's been..." She stumbled over the words.

"For who? You? Really? You think I have no idea what it's like to be alone and to lose one of the most important people in your life?" The heavy veil that had hampered my every breath since Dad died seemed to ignite from my anger, and suddenly, I saw clearly. "I have no idea what it's like to face mean, bitchy people who make fun of you and call your family losers and crazy? I have no idea what it's like to be lost and scared?"

Mom's face was ghostly white, with no expression. A corpse of a mother.

I stepped closer, the ashes of the dark veil smoldering. I felt calm with the white-hot truth. "Mom, I can tell you what doesn't help." I took a breath. "It doesn't help watching you fall apart."

There wasn't anything else to say. I walked past her blank stare and went to my room, exhausted. My heart, my arm and my soul bled.

Chapter 19

I curled into a ball on my bed and cried until I gasped in spasms. Exhausted, I stared at the wall from my damp, salty pillow waiting for night to come.

Tink.

I sat up and wiped dried salt off my face with the back of my hand. I felt like a used rag, and sank back on my bed, with a glance at the clock. Seven? I had slept for over an hour.

Tink. A noise from the side window.

What the—? That wasn't a tree. My cramps throbbed, so I slowly stood and looked out window. Nothing unusual. I opened the window and leaned out into the evening's hums and chirps.

Something moved from behind the tree!

"Hey who's there?" I croaked, my voice hoarse from all the crying and screaming.

"Hey, Alli." Eric stepped out from behind the tree.

"Eric?" *This can't be happening!*

"I missed you in English today." He looked down and kicked some leaves.

Heat flushed my cheeks. "I had a stomach ache, so my mom came and got me."

"Yeah, that's what Ginny Brooks said."

"Oh, good." I felt like my face was on fire.

"I, ah, brought your books."

"What?"

"Ginny brought these to English." He stepped back behind the tree and pulled out the books I had left in Consumer Science.

"Oh, yeah."

"Are you too sick to come and get them?"

"No. I think it was something I ate at breakfast. I feel much better now."

He smiled, put his hand on his chest and sighed. "That's good."

That was kind of weird. "I'll meet you in the front yard."

I shut the window and saw my ring. *Of course! The ring!* I covered my mouth and screamed into my hands and breathlessly took a quick look in the mirror. "Oh, God." I de-tangled my hair, and ran to the bathroom where I rubbed my teeth with toothpaste and splashed cold water on my face.

I kissed my ring, ran down the stairs and stopped. I needed to gather my courage and not look like a raving fool, so I took a deep breath, and I slowly opened the door. "Hey." My new southern twang slipped out as I stepped onto the front porch.

"I'm really sorry about this morning." Eric shifted on his feet.

"What?"

"You know, when I upset you at your locker this morning."

"Oh, no. Really?" I gulped trying to make sense of this. "You just surprised me, and I got caught on my locker." That didn't sound right. My ears had to be fuchsia.

"I know this will sound stupid, but I thought maybe you left school today because of me."

"Oh no." I couldn't tell him the truth. "Really, I had a stomach ache. That's all."

He bit his lip, like he wanted to say something.

"Thanks for bringing my books. I need to study my lines."

He smiled and handed me the books. "I missed you today in English. It wasn't any fun without you." So much for what Margot had said.

Warmth bubbled up from my stomach. "Thanks." A very awkward silence passed.

Eric stared at his feet. *Say something!* "How did you get here?"

"My brother gave me a ride. He's at the Thomases'."

"Cheryl knows you're here?"

"I dunno. Who cares?"

"Do you think Travis will say anything?" That would be a total disaster.

"I don't care if she knows I'm here." Eric's eyebrows pinched together and his smile vanished.

Terrorment seized my ability to think clearly.

"Well, I should get going." He reached out and touched my arm. "I'm glad you're feeling better."

He's touching me! He's warm, soft and beautiful. Keep breathing. "Thanks again for bringing my books. That was so nice of you. Even though you scared me to death." I smiled, trying to recover from the tingly feeling he left on my arm.

"I wasn't sure that was your window, I was about to try the next one when you opened it." He laughed.

"Now you know." I turned and walked to my door.

"See ya, Juliet."

"Bye, Romeo." I shut the door and found Lisa sitting by the dining room window.

"What are you looking at?" I narrowed my eyes, smiling.

"Oh, nothing—Juliet." We both squealed with delight illuminating the darkness that had collected in every corner of our house.

"Shhh." Our laughter seemed so out of place, I felt guilty. "Where's Mom?"

"One guess. Rhymes with dead."

Chapter 20

The next morning, my cramps weren't as bad as I ran for the bus. I was the last on the bus, as planned, and sat in the closest seat to the front. I spied Margot and Cheryl sitting together in the back seat. I stared down at the ring. *Please just let me get to school without a scene.* On my best day, I was no match for either one of them, and their evil combined was simply terrifying. *Help me, dragonfly. It's just me and you against a double dose of 3B.* I could actually feel the hate rays on the back of my head as we bounced our way to school. I was a sitting duck, but there was no way I was going to turn my head and see what they were up to. I kept my eye contact on the only source of hope I had. "Please protect me," I whispered.

In Consumer Science the lights were dimmed as I slid into my seat. Mrs. Moore fiddled with the DVD machine. *Don't flub up a simple movie.* A movie was perfect to sit and chill.

"Are you okay?" Ginny asked as I set my books down.

"Oh, yeah. I feel much better today."

"What happened? Did you barf?"

"No." I swallowed and whispered, "Horrible cramps."

She raised her eyebrows. "Feeling better today?"

"Yeah, thanks."

She nodded and her eyes widened. "After you left, Eric Prinz asked me where you were."

I tried to fight my smile by contorting my lips and biting the inside of my cheek.

"He asked if you were sick, and I said I thought so because you left for the bathroom and never came back. Honestly, Alli, he looked pretty upset."

The view's great up here on cloud nine! "Did you give him my books?"

"No," Ginny grabbed my wrist and leaned in, our noses practically touching. "He asked for them. I think he is going to give you them in English."

"No." My voice went up to a squeal. "He brought them to my house."

Ginny's eyes went wide and she covered her mouth. "You're kidding."

Mrs. Moore looked our way, frowning.

I pretended to pay attention to the stupid movie about kitchen fires and my mind wandered to last night and Eric's perfect green eyes and warm hands. He was so sweet, so romantic. Nervous happiness fluttered around my stomach.

Oh, gentle Romeo if you do love me, pronounce it faithfully,

Or if you think I am won too quickly (and act like Cheryl, the slut),

I'll frown, and be stubborn (like Margot the witch),

And say no to you so you will woo (but that would be too much like Cheryl, the slut).

But in truth, dear Romeo, I am too fond and you will break my heart

But I promise dear Romeo, I will prove to be true and honest (unlike Margot, the wretched witch).

I don't have the heart to play games with you (like Margot and Cheryl would).

I'm afraid you know of my love before I was really ready.

Please don't treat this like casual love.

The bell rang and startled me. "Cripes."

"Let's go, Juliet." Ginny gathered her books.

Did she just read my mind?

####

"Ladies and gentlemen." Mrs. Nottingham stood in the middle of class with her arms folded and her brow furrowed. Once everyone quieted down, she held up a piece of paper. "I am holding the invitation for you to take home. I am reluctant to give it out, because I don't think we are going to be ready to put this on in one week. One week. Next Monday is open house, and I am inviting your families to come and watch what a wonderful job you are doing interpreting Act II, but I personally don't want to be embarrassed. It's up to you and it is going to be decided today." She sighed and looked tired. "You are going to have to convince me that you are serious about this, because I refuse to be publicly humiliated. I'll grade you in class and be done with it."

Eric stood up in his blue T-shirt. "Mrs. Nottingham?"

Mrs. Nottingham raised her eyebrows. "Yes, Eric."

"I'm very serious about doing this. You've made English fun. Scene II is cool." He looked at me. "I know how Romeo feels when he sees Juliet." He walked over to me and took my hand. "But wait, what light comes through that window? It is the east and Juliet is the sun! Arise there sun and chase away the jealous moon; the moon is already sick, umm because—aahhh—" He still gripped my hand.

Stunned, I looked around the room at wide eyes and lots of hands over mouths. Margot's mouth hung open, and I pulled my hand out of Eric's.

"Well, Eric, that's impressive, even if it's not exactly right," Mrs. Nottingham said.

"Wait," Eric interrupted, "I'm not finished." He grabbed my hand again and locked his emerald peepers right into my heart. "The last line is the best. It's something like, Juliet, you are so much more beautiful than the moon or stars or anything else in the world."

My mouth fell open. I was horrified. No, thrilled. Thrillified! I was one hundred percent thrillified.

"Well. Yes, that's close, but not quite right." Mrs. Nottingham stepped in between us and gently pushed us apart. "Very enthusiastic, Eric. And quite realistic." She lingered on the word *quite* and sighed. "Mr. Prinz, we're going to wait for stage directions from now on, okay? And oh, by the way, it's '*arise fair sun,*' as in pretty, '*and chase away the envious moon.*'"

"Oh, that's even better." Eric smiled at Mrs. Nottingham. She chuckled.

My feet loosened slightly from where I stood frozen, but still I felt bewildered as several kids giggled along with Mrs. Nottingham.

"Yes, well, Shakespeare thought so." She turned to the class. "Okay, grab the invitations on the way out of class. Let's start from the beginning of Act II, chorus line up over by the chalkboard."

Eric looked at me and said, "Better get moving, Juliet."

"Oh, Romeo. You deserve an Oscar for that performance," Margot said as she walked over to us.

"It wasn't hard at all." He winked at me and walked over to the chalkboard.

I flushed, still frozen in the same spot.

"Wait until Cheryl hears about this," Margot said with her arms crossed and her head cocked to one side.

My stomach plunged as if I were on a rollercoaster. "I don't know how we were ever friends." She had just completely burst my bubble of joy. "Go tell the buck-toothed trollop. You two deserve each other." I flicked my wrist in her face, waving her off.

The ring caught her attention. "What's that?"

"I found the ring."

Her face betrayed her staunch body language. She was impressed; even with her arms crossed and her mouth pursed, her eyes flickered with awe.

"Pretty cool, don't cha think?" I put my hand out and wiggled my finger. "It fits perfectly. Like it was *made* for me."

Chapter 21

Mom and Mrs. Williamson both looked up from the table as I walked in the kitchen.

Why is she here? I gulped. "Hey, Mrs. Williamson. What's up?"

"Alli, how are you? Your mom and I were just chatting."

Mom peered up at me from her teacup with familiar wet streaks down her face. There was a pile of used tissues next to her, indicating that this discussion had been going on for a while.

"Alli, why don't you have a seat?" She pointed to a chair. "Your mom and I were talking about how things have been for the last few weeks."

Why now? "Does this have anything to do with the fight Margot and I had?"

"Well, I will say that was the incident that made me want to talk to your mom."

I am not going down for this. "Mrs. Williamson, things have been kind of, well, *hard* around here since Dad died." Mom kept her gaze on the teaspoon in front of her.

Mrs. Williamson gently reached over and grabbed my hand. "Alli, I can't imagine how hard life must be for you guys. Everyone must be struggling terribly."

"I can handle most things. It would be fine except Margot told June that our house is haunted and freaked out Lisa!" My voice broke, but I clenched my teeth to keep from falling apart. I didn't want Mom to think I couldn't take it—then I'm sure we'd be packing our bags.

"That was awful of Margot, and she's in very hot water for her behavior."

Hot water? I can't believe this! "It's more than just that. She's been so mean to everyone in my family since, well, *then*, and treating *me* like crap. Like this is my fault or something."

"Honey, Margot has never been faced with a tragedy like this. She loved your dad. He was special to everyone." She pulled her hand away and dabbed her eyes. "He was a wonderful man. I know she hasn't handled this well. I should have done something a long time ago."

"I wish *someone* would do something." I knew I would taste blood if I bit my lip any harder. *Keep it together, Alli.* "Margot's been to this house once and made us all feel like a freak show!" The dam inside of me broke, and the pain flooded out.

"Oh, Alli, Janet, I am so sorry, she has such a terrible way of dealing with stress. How has Lisa been?"

"It took a few days for her to catch up on the school that she missed, but all in all, she's doing better than the rest of us," Mom said.

131

Oh my God! I couldn't believe what I just heard. "No. No, actually that's not true." Mrs. Williamson was a life boat; Mom was the *Titanic*. "Lisa's terrified that Mom is really falling apart and then will really leave; not just locked behind the closed door upstairs." I didn't know if Mom could help sinking, but I wasn't going down, too. Do you know what it's like to have to jump in cold water and swim for a little life boat that has started to leave without you because your own Mother Ship has sunk itself? "Lisa needs me to help her with homework every day." I softened my voice, "But more than that she needs me to tell her things will be okay."

Mom put her head down. "I'm lost. I honestly don't know what to do; maybe I should follow my dad's advice and move back to Connelsville."

"Mom." I covered my mouth before I said something unforgivable. In a controlled voice I said, "Please stop acting so helpless. We're going to be okay."

"Janet, have you considered seeing someone to help you through this extremely difficult situation?"

"I hadn't thought about it," Mom mumbled.

"I mean, honestly, not only do you have to deal with the stress and tragedy of the death of your husband, but you also need to learn how to handle raising two girls all by yourself."

"I don't know, Elaine. I haven't the slightest idea who I would go to or what I would say."

"The guidance department at my school has the number of several grief counselors. That is what they do. Help people deal with grief," she said.

Mom sniffed and played with the used tissues. "I guess it couldn't hurt."

"That's a good idea, Mom. Just talking to someone might help." I smiled at Mrs. Williamson and reached out and touched her arm. "Thanks."

She pursed her lips, trying to smile in a reassuring way, but the edges of her mouth didn't turn up. She patted my hand, instead. "That's lovely."

I glanced at Mom and she raised her eyebrows and shrugged slightly. "It's a ring I found up in my Nana's stuff."

"It's so unique. It looks beautiful on you."

"So, Elaine, do you think you could call me with the name of those counselors?" Obviously, Mom wanted to change the subject.

"Yes, of course. I'll call you tomorrow. I'd better get going." She pushed back from the table and opened her arms to me. She kissed me on the cheek then whispered in my ear, "Maybe the ring will give you strength."

I clung to her warm, comforting embrace and felt my spirit lighten. Meanwhile, Mom just sat there, hypnotized by soggy tissues.

Chapter 22

Lisa and I sat at the dining room table after dinner, studying for the spelling test she had on Wednesday.

"Reluctant," I said.

"R-E- L." She nibbled her nail. "Is the word *luck* in the middle of it? Like *good luck?*"

"Yeah, but there no 'k' like in luck. And a 't' sound follows."

The house phone rang.

"I'll get it." Lisa jumped up and ran around the corner. She giggled as she poked her head into the dining room. "It's a boy."

I reached for the phone with a shaky hand. "Hello?"

"Hi, Alli. It's Eric."

"Oh. Hi, Eric. What's up?" *How did he get my number? Did he Google our address?*

"Well, I was wondering if you would like to practice our lines or something."

"Oh." Excitement and terror clouded my ability to think.

"Well, I mean, we only have a week to remember a lot of

lines. The balcony scene is a killer."

"Yeah, I know what you mean."

"My brother is always over at the Thomases'. He could drop me off some day, you know, if that's cool."

"Oh. Um, yeah. I think that would be okay—how about Wednesday after school?" *That would give me time to clean the house and ask Mom.*

"That's cool." He paused. "Well, good. I'll see ya then."

"I'll probably see you tomorrow in class."

"Oh, yeah." He laughed sounding embarrassed. "Well, see you in English then."

"Bye, Eric." I hung up the phone, my heart pounding. *A thousand times goodnight.*

Wednesday morning, I dusted and wiped up after everything I did. *Is there any way to clean up a mother? I hope she showers today.*

"Believe," I said to Lisa as I loaded the dishwasher.

"B-e-l-i-e-v-e," Lisa said through her cereal.

"You'll do great today."

"Are you wearing mascara?"

"Maybe."

"Does Mom know?"

"Please, don't make me laugh." I opened the kitchen door and blinked my extended lashes at her.

"Have a good day, Alli. You look really pretty."

"Good luck on the spelling test today!" Moist, warm air met me as I walked across the yard. *Great, this humidity will*

135

ruin the lashes. A familiar yellow Mustang stopped across the street.

Travis leaned out his window. "Hey, Alli. Want a ride to school?" Eric waved at me from the back seat.

What? This can't be happening. Go with it, Alli,—even if it's a dream, don't wake up. "Oh. Sure. Thanks." I became acutely aware that my lashes stuck a little as I blinked. I sucked in my belly and some nerve, wiped under my eyes, and treaded through my mile-high grass to the hottest car in the world. *Don't trip, look cool. Forget the wet grass marks on your pants. Leave your eyes alone, you fool.*

"Eric saw you walking out of your house and screamed for me to stop." Travis laughed as I opened the door.

"I didn't scream." Eric glared at his brother.

"Hey, Alli." MGM's brown eyes and velvety Greek-god voice shook me to the core.

"Hey, Matt." I slid onto the cool back seat and felt giddy as spicy and sweet colognes swirled around me. I wiped my eyes again and shifted in my seat. "Jeez, I hope I didn't track in any mud or anything." *You are such a loser! Shut up!*

"When I saw you walking out of your house, I thought, what the heck—right?" Eric shrugged his shoulders and smiled.

We pulled to the corner, and I watched Cheryl's face plummet as she caught a glimpse of me in the backseat. She slapped Margot on the shoulder and pointed to the car, yelling the whole time. Margot's face twisted from shocked to angry as she rubbed her shoulder.

I felt like Miss America waving to the crowd, then

noticing someone pointing a gun at me.

MGM slapped the dashboard and hooted. "Did you see the look on my loser sister's face?"

"I sure did." I fake laughed.

"Don't worry about her. She's all bark, no bite."

Yeah, right.

####

Eric walked me to Consumer Science looking and smelling delicious. "Can I meet you here and walk you to English?"

"Sure. Thanks again for everything." I floated into class and sat next to Ginny.

"Was that Eric Prinz?"

"Yeah. He, his brother and Matt Thomas drove me to school today."

"Oh my God."

I couldn't help but raise my eyebrows and nod at her in agreement. Yes, in fact, I had just experienced the coolest thing ever. I completely ignored whatever Mrs. Moore babbled about and focused on the clock. The desperately slow, ticking clock. I must have twirled the dragonfly ring a hundred times when the bell finally rang. I walked out and saw Eric jogging down the hall.

"Hey, ready?" He smiled, catching his breath.

"Yeah. You don't have to walk me everywhere, you know."

"You don't want me to?"

"No, it's not that. I just don't want you to be late or anything."

"No worries, Juliet."

Someone pinch me. Seriously.

We walked to English and there, talking outside the classroom, were the devil and her hand-maiden. Almost as if they were waiting for us. "Oh, no," I mumbled.

"I thought she might show up," Eric said.

I gulped and tried to ignore the hate stares coming from the dynamic-dumb duo.

We walked to the doorway and Cheryl chirped, "Hey Eric, how come you didn't give me a ride to school today?" She flashed a sickly, over-glossed smile at him and twirled her hair.

"We didn't have any room."

Mrs. Nottingham called, "Let's go, folks! Time's a-wasting!"

Nick tried to make his way into the classroom. "Excuse me lovely ladies," he said.

"Get lost, loser," Margot said.

"Who was that? Cheryl asked.

"Nick Klark." Margot gave Cheryl the thumbs down sign.

"Nick's a really nice guy," Eric said, stepped back and let me go through the door first, but I couldn't help glance back at Cheryl. She was peering into the room checking out Nick! She caught me looking at her, and now I knew what the phrase *If looks could kill* meant.

"Time is money, people." Mrs. Nottingham stood in the middle of the room surrounded by huge boxes.

"It's time, lords and ladies, to change our humble abode into the bard's Verona."

I loved Mrs. Nottingham, but honestly, she was always throwing a word or two into every sentence that confused the heck out of me. "We're going to use these boxes to build an orchard, a balcony and something that will look like Friar Lawrence's cell. There are brushes, scissors and paint over by my desk. I want to see everyone working on something. We only have today and tomorrow to get this place looking like Verona. Then Friday's final rehearsal."

I went to the sink to clean some glue off the scissors, and put my ring on the counter so I wouldn't get any gook on it.

"Well, you certainly know how to make an enemy." Margot stood behind me.

"Who are you talking about? You or Cheryl?"

Margot picked up the ring and slipped it on. "Seriously, Alli. I don't get it. Now that you've got this voodoo ring, you're acting like you're too good for everybody."

Oh my God. She's got the ring! I fought a panic rattling its way up my chest. "Give that back, right now." My voice quivered.

Margot smirked. "I kind of like it on me." She held her hand out admiring *my* ring.

"Give. It. Back." I felt tears welling. "Please."

I felt my mojo slipping away. I had no power, Cinderella after midnight.

She narrowed her eyes and took a step closer to me. "Why should I?"

What a royal 3B. "Margot. I'll tell Mrs. Nottingham and you'll be in more trouble with her."

"I'll tell." She mocked. "Seriously?" She took off my ring

139

and put it in my sweaty palm. "Here ya go Spaz. Don't get your panties all bunched up."

I slipped the ring on and took a deep breath. "Why don't you go have a cigarette with your buddy?"

"Hey, Alli. Want to help me?" Eric had perfect timing.

Eric and I each worked on a tree for the balcony scene. He created a lovely tree with branches on it, and mine looked like a big Q-Tip. "Your tree looks so nice. Mine looks like a first grader made it." I said, while watching Margot's every move.

"Here let me help you cut some branches or something." Eric tippy-toed over to my cardboard tree. "Like this." He started cutting into the big ball that was supposed to be the tree top, artfully adding realistic looking branches.

I tried to copy his movement, but my branch had no character. I put down the scissors and tried to tear a few natural looking curves into the branch, but instead ripped the branch off. "Oh, crap." The bell rang as I stared at the damage.

"Hey, I've got gym next, so I better run, but I'll see you later at your house, right? Eric picked up the scissors from the floor. "Looks like you don't need these."

I laughed. "Yep, seems like I can ruin something with my bare hands."

"You just don't know your own strength." His mouth curled at one corner and a dimple-appeared.

Only when I'm wearing my ring.

140

Chapter 23

I threw my backpack down, scanned the kitchen for dirty dishes and saw a note from Mom saying she'd be back soon; she had an appointment with Steve, a counselor. *That's a good sign.* So, there was time to get things looking decent. Okay—first me, then the house. I ran upstairs and de-gunked my braces. While brushing my teeth, I noticed pit stains. I raised my arms and saw wet marks the size of apples saturating my shirt with loser juice. *Gross.* I tugged it off (carefully avoiding the *moisture)* and snagged my ring on a button hole. *The ring, of course. Relax. You've got people looking out for you.* I yelled, "Thank you," hoping that someone or *something* would happen—like a flickering light, a book drop or even a friendly, "You're welcome."

Nothing.

Nothing but the house's familiar, lonely silence. *Focus. Eric's coming soon!* My stomach flickered with nerves as if sending Morse code to my brain. *You're way out of your league, sister!* I doused my self doubt with a healthy squirt of perfume and ran downstairs to unload the dishwasher. I peeked out the window as Travis's Mustang pulled up.

Oh God, he's here. My fingers felt like ice and my throat like a desert. I put my head under the faucet in the bathroom and took a last minute check in the mirror. *I really do look like a dead worm. Eric's going to see me and run from the house screaming.* I walked toward the door, trying to muster some spit and some kind of game. I twirled the ring, as if mustering up some confidence. I needed to focus on something besides the fact that Eric Prinz was about to enter my house, and I might die from nerves.

"Hey." Eric walked up to me as Travis honked and drove away.

"Hey." I smiled. "Um, where's your English book?" *Did my voice just quiver? Pull it together!*

"Oh." He looked at his feet.

"Is it in your brother's car?"

"No. I left it at home."

"Well, I guess we can share. I think I have most of my lines down."

"Alli?" He looked out to the yard and then put his hands in his pockets. "I really came here to ask you something."

"Oh really?" My voice definitely trembled.

"Well, I wondered... um." He looked like he'd seen a ghost.

This is going to be bad. "Are you okay?"

His eyes looked watery and he was very pale. "No. I mean, yes. I'm okay." He sighed and shook his head. "This isn't coming out right."

"Is it bad?"

"I hope you don't think so."

It's bad.

"I wondered if you wanted to go out with me."

"You want me to go out with you? Like to the movies or something?"

"No. Oh, yes. I would like to go to the movies with you, but I meant as, you know, like my girlfriend." Eric's cheeks flushed bright red as if he had just run a mile at full speed. "Alli, I don't know any fancy words like Romeo uses, but honestly, I know what he felt when he saw Juliet across the room."

"Really?" *Breathe. Breathe.*

"Yeah. You walked into class and all I could think was that you were really, really cute." He shifted on his feet and let out a deep breath.

I wet my lips. My heart pounded.

He smiled and touched my arm. "I think you're beautiful."

"Oh, thanks. I think you're beautiful too." *You idiot! Recover, recover!* "Well. I mean, I do think you're beautiful. Your heart—and your eyes."

A gentle smile warmed his face. He leaned closer. An invisible magnet pulled me toward him. His lips brushed mine. He looked at me, and I felt the warmth of his breath as he slowly pressed his soft, moist lips against mine. Soft, soft, moist, wonderful lips. My knees went soggy, and something deep in my soul melted. A tear snuck out the side of my eye, as if my heart were literally overflowing. Then, of course I ruined it when my braces bashed into his teeth. *You spaz!* I jumped away from him.

"I'm sorry, Alli. I don't know what I was thinking. I shouldn't have kissed you."

"No, no, it's not that." I wiped my eye. "That was really nice." My nose dribbled, and I quickly wiped it with the back of my hand.

"Oh." Eric sighed and smiled. "I thought so too."

Mom's car turned into the driveway and the same invisible magnet that pulled me toward him repelled us apart. She stepped out of the car with her eyebrows raised.

"Ah, Mom, this is Eric Prinz." *Did she see us kiss?*

"Hello, Eric. So you're Romeo?" She held a grocery bag with one hand and reached in the mailbox and pulled out today's flyers and bills with her other.

"Yes, ma'am." He put his hands in his pocket, and I noticed a curl stuck on his glistening forehead.

What did she mean by that?

"I'm sorry I'm late getting here, I hope I didn't miss too much." She cocked her head a little and looked at me.

She saw.

"I stopped at the store for a few things to make cookies."

"Cookies?" I couldn't help the surprised sound in my voice.

"Yeah, cookies." Mom narrowed her eyes, as if to say, "Watch it, kid, I know what you were doing."

"Thanks, Mom. I guess your *meeting* went well?"

"It was a good beginning." She opened the kitchen door, and we followed her in. I grabbed my English book. "We'll be in the living room, okay?"

"Nice meeting you, Mrs. Collins." Eric followed me

around the corner into the living room.

"Ah, she doesn't make cookies very often. This is some special day. That is, my mom isn't much of a baker."

"Cool." Eric smiled as he wiped the *moisture* off his forehead.

Lisa opened the kitchen door and yelled, "I'm home." She poked her head around the corner into the living room. "Hi."

"Hey, Lisa. This is Eric." I tried to play it cool.

"Hi Eric," she said in a sing-song voice.

"Hey."

"Okay, Lisa. We really need to practice, so maybe you could go and help Mom or something?"

"With the cookies?"

"Yep."

"I'll call you guys when they're ready." She turned the corner and popped back around just enough for me to see her and mouthed, *He's so cute.*

I tried to ignore her and focused on Eric. "Okay, you start Scene II where I'm on the balcony." I plopped down on the couch with the English book.

"He jests at scars that never found a wound."

"Eric, it's not *found.* It's *felt.*"

"I don't understand this stuff." He sighed. "Stupid words like *jest* and *thou* are killing me."

"The line is, 'He jests at scars that never felt a wound.' Romeo means that people who have never been in love can laugh at those who have because they don't know what it feels like."

"He—I—never even mentions love. And who's the *he?* Am *I* the *he?*"

"No. You're not the *he;* Mercutio and Benvolio are the *he.* Well I guess it should be *they* or *those,* but hang with me here. Mercutio and Benvolio are the *he* Romeo is talking to. How about if I try to paraphrase this section for you?" He stared at me—maybe he didn't know what *paraphrase* meant. Nana told me what paraphrasing was because she always needed to explain what the priest was saying when I went with her to mass. "Okay. So, this is how Romeo might say the line in today's language. Those losers don't know what it's like to be in love because they have never felt the pain of love."

"I'm never going to get this." Eric sank into the cushion next to me. "It sure makes sense when you say it." He grinned at me, and I absolutely felt love's dagger prick my heart.

"Well, maybe you don't have to understand every line, but just get the meaning behind it."

"I like it when you tell me what it means." He looked at me. *Zing.* Cupid's arrow or Romeo's dagger; whatever *it* was pierced me. I could barely catch my breath, and the room seemed to swirl around us. Time flew or stood still (who cares?) when Eric's sea green eyes—framed by dark, lush, perfectly gorgeous lashes—gazed at me as I babbled on about Romeo's lines. He smiled and nodded, and I got all woozy when his pinchable, sweet dimples lit up his cheeks. Juliet's lines? NO PROBLEMO.

Eric sighed.

"You're getting it, right?"

"Only when you explain it to me." He rubbed his face with his hands and sighed. "Why can't they talk normal, like you? *That*, I get. I totally get it when you explain it. You make it chill."

I make it chill! "Well, I'm just paraphrasing. You know, using my own words to explain what I think Shakespeare meant."

"Can I paraphrase instead of learn my lines?"

"I don't think so."

"Well, I think everyone would like this stuff better if we could just talk in normal English."

How's this for normal English? You're gorgeous. Please kiss me again.

Lisa came around the corner. "Alli. Can you come into the kitchen?" Lisa's tone made it clear something was wrong and I automatically started moving toward the kitchen.

The sweet smell of baking cookies reached me before I saw Mom sobbing at the kitchen table holding an envelope.

"What's wrong Mom?"

"The bill."

"The bill?"

"For Dad's funeral."

"Oh." I took the envelope and sighed. Pain was even delivered by mail.

I didn't want Eric to see this. Couldn't she hold it together for once—for me?

"Mom. Come, on." I rubbed my face, trying to figure out how to get her upstairs without Eric noticing.

"I'll finish the cookies. Just go upstairs and rest."

Eric would never come back if he saw how we really were. Broken.

"Everything okay?" He asked after I walked back into the living room.

"My mom doesn't feel very well." I stared at the rug.

"Oh. Well, Maybe I should probably get going."

I nodded, feeling bad that Eric was leaving, and mad at Mom. "Let me give you some cookies for the road." I handed him four warm cookies as he opened the door.

"Walk with me, will ya?" We stepped out onto the driveway.

"I need to take the next batch of cookies out of the oven in a minute."

"Okay." He looked around. "Looks like your yard could use some help."

"Yeah. No one has touched it since my grandfather was here a few weeks ago." *For Dad's funeral.* My throat tightened, and I coughed. "The yard was really my dad's thing." I swallowed, blinking back tears, and then whispered, "I know it looks terrible. It's hard to, you know, just get the mower out. It's silly. I know."

"Alli, I'm so sorry about your dad." He reached out and rubbed my arm. "It must suck so bad."

"It does." I wiped the tears out of my eyes and sniffed. *Do not start bawling.* "I'll get to the yard this weekend."

Eric nodded and stared at his shoes.

"Well, listen. I'll call ya. Okay?"

"Sure."

"Thanks for everything, Alli." He dimpled, I mean

smiled and world paused for one beautiful second.

Lisa giggled when I walked in.

"What?"

"He's nice," Lisa said through a mouth full of cookie.

"Yeah. Nice." *Nice and gorgeous.* "I'm going to take some cookies up to Mom."

"Mom?" I knocked on her door. "I brought you a couple of cookies." Mom's face was a horrible mixture of tears and snot. A complete mess-lost and desperate.

I needed to snap her out of this. Lisa was freaking out downstairs. "So, good meeting with Steve today?"

She sniffed and sat up. "I'll be talking to him for a long time, I think." She was talking to me like I was the Mom. "One thing Steve made clear is that I can't do this alone."

"That's for sure." *I've got the ring. But what do you have?*

"I've got some good news."

"Yeah?" I could really use some.

"Grandma and Pap are coming to see you in the play."

"Awwh. That makes me more nervous."

"Don't be silly, Alli. They planned on coming for the weekend, and now they're going to stay to see the play. That's all."

"I'm going downstairs to clean up." *Your mess.*

September 18th

Dear Diary,

I would like this red to be Alli Collins' blood from where I clawed her face off. That slut has thrown herself at Eric, and he's fallen for it.

Eric showed up at our house tonight looking for Travis. I heard his voice and went into the kitchen. Mom said she didn't know that Travis drove him over and Eric said he had been up at Alli Collins' house. I could not believe what I was hearing!!!

Why does he want to be at the loser's house? Why can't he see how much I love him? We're supposed to be together. His beautiful green eyes should be looking at me and not that gross idiot up the street.

I've been in my room crying for an hour. I guess they're gone because I heard a car leave our driveway a while ago. I've been crying so hard I've made Jelly Beans all wet. His velvet ears feel gross. Nothing helps. I want to die. No, I take that back. It's not me I want to die.

Chapter24

Friday night I stood in front of my mirror practicing my lines.

*"Love's heralds should be thoughts, which ten times faster glide than the sun's beams driving back shadows over low' ring hills. Therefore do nimble opinioned doves...*um, doves have opinions" I checked my English book. "Oh. It's *pinion'd doves*—what's that?" I fell back on my bed. "I am not going to get this by Monday." *Eric's right. Some lines don't make any sense.*

Eric hadn't caught on to most of the lines, yet. He was drowning in Lake Shakespeare, and Mrs. Nottingham didn't want to give swimming lessons anymore. She sighed loudly or rubbed her head every time he flubbed up his lines, which was often.

"Eric, it's a play on words! Mercutio and Romeo are joking about the goose. There isn't a real goose in the scene."

"But, what about when I say, 'nay good goose, bite not?'"

"You're talking to Mercutio. Not a real goose! Have you been paying attention the last two weeks at all?" She had left class several times saying she was giving herself a time-out, but even that didn't seem to help. She would return from her time-outs with the same deep crease in her forehead and, if possible, with even less of a sense of humor than before.

My temples pounded, and I stared at the ceiling. *That's enough.* I had to mow the lawn before Grandma and Pap arrived tomorrow. I took the ring off and put it in the black box. *"By and by, I come-To cease thy suit and leave me to my grief. To-morrow I will send."* I kissed the box thinking of Eric. *"A thousand times goodnight!"*

####

The morning sun blinded me as I sat up and looked out my window. I rubbed my eyes and shook my head to focus. *No way.* I looked again and yes, one of the most beautiful sights known to any fourteen-year-old girl dazzled in front of me— Matt Thomas without his shirt mowing the lawn! But he was on *my* lawn—mowing—without his shirt on. *What's going on?* I jumped out of bed, threw on the jeans, bra and shirt that were on the floor and ran downstairs. I opened the door and found Travis and Eric weeding the flowerbed by the front door.

"Hey. What's all this?" My stomach plunged as if I were on a rollercoaster—thrillified.

"This yard needs more than one girl." Travis looked up smiling and wiped the sweat off his brow.

I looked at Eric, trying to make sense of this. "Are you guys kidding? I can't believe how nice this is." His smile flooded me with warm tingles. As soon as I opened my mouth, I realized I hadn't brushed my teeth—or hair. *Crap.*

I ran my hand over my hair. *There are a couple of beauties, and I'm a beast.*

Mom walked out behind me in her nightgown. "Well, what's this?"

"Hi, Mrs. Collins." Matt stopped the lawn mower. "I've noticed your yard could use a little attention. I hope you don't mind." He pulled his T-shirt out of his back pocket and put it on.

"Matt Thomas. Well, I never." Her voice cracked a little, and she shook her head. Her eyes wandered to Eric and Travis. "My goodness. Hello, Eric."

"Hi, Mrs. Collins. This is my brother, Travis."

"Travis is my best friend," Matt clarified.

"Oh, for heaven's sake." She nodded like she understood the connection. "You boys." Mom blinked several times, as if the sun was in her eyes, but I knew that wasn't it. "Honestly, you don't know how wonderful this is."

"It's no problem," Matt said. "Matter of fact, well, if you don't mind, I'll mow every once in a while, you know, when I notice it might need it."

"I couldn't ask you to do that," Mom said.

Lisa peeked out from behind Mom's nightgown, her eyes big as saucers.

"Honestly, it's no problem. I can count it as my community service hours for school."

Mom pinched her lips together and nodded. She seemed dazed as she walked back into the house.

"Hey, Alli. Do you want to help me pick up the bush trimmings?" Eric said.

"Ah, sure, just let me go and get something." I really needed to brush my teeth!

I ran upstairs with Lisa on my heels. "Can I help, Alli?" Her messy hair and excited tone reminded me of Christmas morning. As far as I was concerned, this was better than Christmas.

"Sure." I smiled. "Get changed, and come on out."

She squealed and kissed me on the cheek.

I threw my hair into braids, brushed and gargled, and rushed down stairs. I heard Mom on the phone. "Please let your mom know how wonderful and thoughtful he is."

No.

"Thank you, Cheryl. I appreciate that." Mom hung up the phone. I stared at her in disbelief. "Alli. What's the matter?"

"You called the Thomases?"

"I really appreciate Matt's kindness and I thought his mom should know."

I stood and blinked. *My mother just unleashed the devil.*

"For heaven's sake. There are three handsome young men out in our yard. Maybe you should go see if they would like something to drink."

I stepped out onto the front porch, and Eric's eyes softened and a broad smile crossed his face. "Juliet."

The thought of 3B vanished, and warmth pulsed through my chest, radiated up my face and curled my mouth into a smile.

"Ah, hey. Alli?" Travis looked at us, chuckling. "You think you could bring that garbage bag over here?"

"Oh, sure." My cheeks burned. *Pull it together. Get a grip.*

"What do you want?" I heard Matt yell over the lawn mower.

I turned and saw the devil herself in my driveway.

Chapter 25

Margot stood a few feet behind Cheryl on the sidewalk.

"What do you think you're doing?" Cheryl screamed over the mower.

The lawn mower stopped. "You'd better not be talking to me," Matt said flatly.

Cheryl put her hands on her hips and sneered at Eric. Her glare reminded me of the zombies in horror movies that send fiery-red death beams from their eyes to their poor, emerald-eyed victims. "Why are you here?" she said.

Eric stood up and walked several steps closer to her. "I'm helping Alli."

"Why would you help *her*?" She pointed at me. "She's a spastic loser. Her whole family's nuts."

"Cheryl, honest to God. You'd better watch it." Matt's voice became low and menacing. "Turn around and take your nasty—" He took a deep breath, controlling himself. "Leave."

I felt like I was naked in a dream and everyone could see me, but I couldn't run. It was the absolute, worst, fart-in-the-middle-of-the-cafeteria-and-everyone-knows-it-was-you type of feeling.

"Why? Why would anyone help her?" Cheryl's voice wavered ever so slightly. I thought I heard desperation in her voice, although I wasn't sure. That was a completely unfamiliar sound coming from her. She glanced over her shoulder toward, Margot, I assumed looking for support. "She doesn't have any friends. Margot can't even stand to be around her anymore."

Margot didn't even blink. She puckered her lips a little and simply shook her head in a disapproving motion, reminding me of the look she often gave June.

"Margot. Tell them how this place is a dump." Cheryl stomped her foot, and again her voice sounded a little higher pitched than normal, and it came off sounding like begging rather than her usual barking.

Margot met Cheryl's stare. "No." Her eyes shifted to mine and there was softness there. *She missed me.* I saw it for a split second before she pursed her lips and walked away. She wiped something off her cheek with a quick flick of her finger.

Was that a tear?

"Margot. Get back here!" Cheryl screamed with her fists clenched by her sides.

"Leave," Matt said calmly.

I don't remember moving, but somehow I found myself inches from Cheryl's face. "Get off my property."

Her eyes widened so much I saw whites all the way around her black-lined rims. "Don't talk to me, you freakin' spaz."

"Whatever, loser. Why don't you go and have another cigarette?" I kept my eyes locked on her pinched-up, buck-toothed, snotty face. She took a step back, but narrowed her eyes and curled her lip, like an animal backed into a corner.

She's gonna kill me.

"What! Cigarettes? Are you kidding me? Wait 'til Mom and Dad hear about this!" Matt really seemed to be enjoying this.

"You've done it now." Cheryl snarled and stepped closer.

Do your best, Vomitosa.

"She's lying!" Cheryl yelled inches from my face. She had so much mascara and liner on, she looked a little like a wild Betty Boop—*with bad breath.* "No one believes anything she says. She's nuts." Cheryl snickered. "She actually thinks Eric's her boyfriend."

"I am her boyfriend." Eric came and stood next to me.

Cheryl's eyes narrowed into slits, and her mouth squeezed together into a thin line. I thought she might explode. "After all we've been through. Our family trips, and—and—she—" Cheryl pointed at me. "She's a slut! She flashed Matt her boob."

Oh my God. I felt like I'd been shot. My knees buckled a little, and I swayed. But then, I took a deep breath, summoned all the power, strength and confidence the ring had given me and stepped closer. "I'm not a slut. I fell off my bike. It was an accident. But nothing you do is on accident, is it? All the times you embarrassed me or tripped me in middle school. Laughing and making fun of me on the bus. None of those things were accidents, were they, Cheryl?" Confidence echoed through my strong and even voice. "You're a mean, horrible, pathetic person and I am sick of you and all your crap. Get-off-my-property."

Her nostrils flared and her eyes widened. I scared her!

Matt walked a few steps closer to us. "You heard the lady. Get off her property."

Cheryl stepped backward onto the sidewalk. "Come on, Eric."

Eric sighed. "Maybe at one time we had a chance, you know, all the camping trips and stuff. Our families are tight, right?"

What's he saying?

He smirked at Matt. "But really, Cheryl. Now that I know you suck your thumb, well, it's ruined it for me."

"What?" She gasped.

"I saw you the other day watching TV, sucking your thumb, rubbing a stuffed rabbit. Now, smoking too? Talk about an oral fixation."

Classic! That explains her buck teeth. This is priceless!

Cheryl staggered back a step, turned and ran away. Then, and I'm not kidding about this, she tripped and fell.

"Jeez, maybe you guys were a bit harsh on her," Travis said.

"What?" Matt and Eric said at the same time.

"I mean, obviously she's just threatened by Alli and Eric's, you know, *friendship,*" Travis said.

Cheryl's threatened by me?

"Travis, are you for real?" Matt shook his head. "That little sister of mine has needed to be smacked down a few pegs for ages." He winked at Eric and me. "Good for you two. She's had that coming for a long time. She may never see the light of day again after I tell my parents that she's smoking. Nice going, Alli." He started up the mower.

Me? I didn't do it. It was the ring. I rubbed my thumb across my ring finger, to twirl my good luck charm, but I didn't feel it. *Where's my ring? Did I drop it? Didn't I put it on this morning?* Did I just tell Cheryl off without wearing the dragonfly ring?

Mom opened the front door. "Who's screaming?"

"Oh, my sister stopped by, and we had to yell over the mower," Matt said.

Mom nodded. Lisa stood next to her with one pig-tail braided.

Time to change the subject. "Lisa, are you going to come and help us or spend all day getting ready?"

"Mom, see? You're taking too long." Lisa said.

"For heaven's sake, Lisa. I wanted you to look nice when Grandma and Pap arrive."

"I'll be right out!" She grabbed Mom's hand and pulled her in the house.

Lisa bounded out of the house a few minutes later and grabbed a trash bag. We had just about picked up all the clippings when Lisa yelled, "They're here."

"Let's get the bags tied up and push off," Matt said to Travis.

"Eric, thank you so much for doing this." I wiped a trickle of sweat off my face.

"I'm glad to help," Eric said.

Lisa ran up to Grandma and Pap's car and wrapped her arms around Grandma's neck before she could even get out of the car. "Goodness, Lisa. What a welcome." She laughed and kissed her on the cheek.

"Mom. Dad." Mom walked out the kitchen door. "You made great time." She looked over at Matt and Travis. "Boys, please let me give you something for your trouble."

"No, honestly, Mrs. Collins. It's not a problem," Matt said.

"Mom and Dad, these young men came over and mowed the grass, cleaned up the hedges and flower beds. They were out here working before the birds were up."

Pap raised his eyebrows. "Out of the goodness of their hearts?"

"Something like that." Mom smiled at me. "This is Eric and Travis Prinz. And this is Matt Thomas from down the street." She added quietly, "Eric and Alli are friends."

"Aha." Pap laughed. "I knew there had to be a reason."

Pap! How could you? I shrugged at Eric, feeling my ears grow hot.

Grandma pulled out a tin foil-lined shoe box. "Could I interest you fellas in some cookies?"

Grandma brought cookies!

"Sure, thanks." Matt and Travis walked over and took a couple. "Nice to meet you." Travis looked over. "Eric, you coming?"

"Yeah." He sighed, looked at the ground, then raised his lush lashes and *zing!* He pierced me with his sparkly, green eyes. "See you later, okay?"

"Okay." *Very clever, Juliet. You sound like a dunce.*

"Eric, please take a few with you." Grandma held out the shoe box.

"Thanks, very much."

"You'd better practice those lines," I yelled as he headed down the street. He turned and waved, chomping on a cookie. *Romeo.*

Grandma batted her eyes. "What a lovely boy."

"He's Romeo in the play," Lisa said.

Grandma laughed. "I hope you two aren't star-crossed lovers."

"Nope." *Everyone's a joker.* "Pap, let me help you with the suitcases." *So I can get away from Grandma who seems to read my mind.*

"Can you help me make some lunch?" Mom asked as I entered the kitchen dragging the suitcases.

"I was hoping to take a shower."

"I'll help you Janet," Grandma said. "Go on up, Alli."

"Thanks, Grandma." I ran upstairs, shut my bedroom door and went straight for the black box on my dresser. I peeked inside and there was the ring, right where I'd left it last night. *I can't believe it.* Never in a million years would I have the nerve to tell Cheryl Thomas off, *especially* without the ring.

I pulled it out of the box, held it up and watched the sunlight sparkle through the wings. *Maybe it has some kind of long-range power or something.* I put it back in the box and headed toward the bathroom. *No, I would have had its power the whole time it was in the attic if that were true. Maybe I have to wear it enough to fill me with a charge or something.* Nothing made sense. I wracked my brain as I lathered, rinsed and dried off. I couldn't figure it out. As soon as I was dressed, I reached for the black box and placed the dragonfly on my finger. *That's better.*

"You want some chips with your sandwich?" Grandma already had her hand in the bag.

"Thanks, Grandma." I sat at the table. "Where's everyone?"

"They're outside checking out the handiwork of your friends."

Joy pinged around in my stomach, sending my mouth involuntarily into a smile. I quickly covered my smile by biting into a ham sandwich, so Grandma wouldn't bust my chops again.

"That was a very nice thing for those young men to do." She sat down next to me. "Did you meet this boy at school?"

"Yep. He's in my English class," I mumbled, keeping the sandwich in front of my mouth, seeing she was going to continue on this subject.

"Well, he certainly has good taste." She noticed the ring on my hand and blinked a couple times. "Where did you get that?"

I ran my tongue over my braces to clear any bready remains. "I found it in Nana Collins' stuff."

"I remember this ring."

I put the sandwich down. "You're kidding."

"No, really. Your Nana wore this ring on your mom and dad's wedding day."

"What?"

"Yup. Your Nana wore all purple to their wedding, and it matched her dress beautifully." She had a faraway look in her eyes as she rubbed my hand. "My goodness. That was a happy day."

"What else do you remember about Nana?"

She stared at the ceiling, as if an old movie of Nana were being shown on the stucco. "Let's see. I remember how proud she was of your dad, and how much she loved your mom. It was a beautiful day."

"I mean, about the ring, Grandma. Do you remember anything about the ring?"

"Oh." She blinked a few times and refocused on me. "Well, she sat with us at dinner, and you know I didn't know her very well back then, so I remember asking her about this ring, to strike up a conversation."

"And?" My heart pounded.

Pap opened the kitchen door followed by Lisa and Mom. "Those boys did a really nice job on the yard." I felt the calluses on Pap's hand as he rubbed my back.

"Janet, we were just talking about Alma's ring. It's been years since I've seen that thing."

Mom sighed. "Not the ring again."

"Grandma says she remembers Nana wearing it to your wedding."

"I don't remember," Mom said point-blank. Clearly, she didn't want to talk about the ring anymore. Or was it the wedding—and Dad—she didn't want to remember?

I didn't want to ruin the happy mood or make Mom mad so I took my dish to the sink. "I think I'll go and study my lines. Can we talk more later, Grandma?"

"Of course," Grandma said.

I went up to my room and pulled the journal out from under my bed. There was one short entry after Nana's trip to Fez. I read it again hoping to find some clue that I may have missed.

November 25

We leave tomorrow. What a trip. It has been such a treat to see Dave and Diane in this magical land. The woman's face from Medina still haunts me. I'm not sure I believe any of that hooey, but I must say the ring is beautiful and will always remind me of my trip. Gotta pack!

Okay, so not even Nana believed the ring possessed special powers, but she did call Morocco magical. I flipped back to November 23. There had to be something else. The ring was meant for me. The old woman said to Nana, "to help you and your daughter on life's journey." The ring was supposed to help me find my "true sense of self." I fanned the pages and inhaled the smell, hoping something would happen, but the powdery smell only reminded me of Nana's house in Gloucester. Now *those* were magical times.

Maybe I could get Grandma to tell me more about the ring without Mom around.

September 21

Dear Diary

    I have to write with black because today started as the absolute worst day of my entire life. It began when Mrs. Collins called our house wanting to tell Mom what a great guy Matt was. God. Another person who thought Matt was the best thing in the world. I told Mrs. Collins that Mom was getting her nails done and she said, "Oh, well, can you tell her to call me when she gets back? I want to tell her how nice it is for Matt, Travis and Eric Prinz to help us out." I almost threw up.

    I called Margot and told her to march her butt up to my house—PRONTO—there was going to be a show-down at Alli's house. She didn't want to go, but I screamed at her and told her she had to come.

    We got to Alli's, and Matt, Travis and Eric all ganged up and yelled at ME. I couldn't believe they defended that slut, even after I told them about Alli's "Girls Gone Wild" stunt.

    It was the worst feeling in the world, and then Eric, my one true friend who always is there for me, out-ed me. He told my most personal secret to the world.

    I ran home and called Margot and wanted to know why she left. Margot told me that she was sick of being mean. She wants to be friends with Alli again. Margot said no one likes me because I'm so mean. I told her the reason I was mean to her was that she dumped me when Alli moved in.

That was all I could take. I hung up the phone and started bawling at the kitchen table when Mom walked in and asked what was going on with all the screaming and crying? I just walked upstairs and she followed me to my room. I showed her JB and told her that I still snuggled with JB. She didn't get it. She said, "What do you mean you still snuggle with JB, like when you were little?" She made it sound sick or something. I said, "You know," and put my thumb near my mouth. Mom didn't say anything, but she got it.

Now I'll change to a grey pen, because it's not as bad as black, but just about. I was at rock bottom and guess what? Mom wasn't mad. She hugged me and told me it was okay. It was a huge relief once Mom knew. She looked at me like I was a real person, and then started crying, saying it was really all her fault.

I couldn't believe it. She said she should have been paying more attention and rubbed my cheek. I know she was looking at my teeth, but she didn't say anything.

I told her I desperately wanted to stop sucking my thumb and if I did, would she please let me get braces? I mean, how bad is that—actually begging to be a brace face?

We walked out to the fire pit in the backyard and

burned Jelly Beans. It was kind of nice, we both said he was a good friend, but we didn't need him anymore. We had each other.

I cried so hard I thought my head was going to pop off. I wasn't sad about JB. I bawled so hard because Mom looked at me as if she really saw me. Me! Mom said we would get through this rough patch together and she would call about an orthodontist appointment on Monday.

Chapter 26

The next morning, I followed the comforting, snuggly smell of coffee that filled our house when my grandparents visited, but I stopped in the hall outside the kitchen when I heard Mom sob.

"Janet, I just want you to consider it."

Mom's voice was low and watery. "Dad, I don't think it would solve any of my problems."

"I would be there to help with the girls and to make sure things were working around the house."

Oh no. Pap is talking about moving again. I leaned forward, straining to hear every word.

"I don't know, Dad. Connelsville isn't home for me anymore."

"But Mom and I would always be around to help watch the girls. I could come and fix a leaky faucet or anything like that. You have to consider the girls; they need a male figure in their lives."

My feet were glued to the floor. *He's going to talk her into it.* I tried to move, but Mom's voice sounded a little stronger and I stopped.

"Maybe you are right."

"Of course I'm right. Come home until you can cope on your own."

Mom blew her nose and scoffed. "When will that be?"

"I dunno, maybe when you're ready to take off your wedding ring."

"My ring? That's funny. I've only started wearing my ring after Walt died. When he was alive, I never bothered. It was just a silly circle on my finger to tell the world my status. The ring didn't change my love or commitment to him." She sighed. It was her sigh; Mom's personal, vapid song that echoed through the house every day. "But then when Walt died, I wanted to wear something that reminded me of our love, our commitment to each other. I don't know if I'll ever want to take it off, Dad."

I never paid any attention to her wearing a ring.

"I know it's just a symbol, but it really comforts me to wear something from him."

That cold, electric feeling flashed through me. I had to put my hand on the wall to steady myself. *That's it! The dragonfly's a symbol of Nana and Dad's love. It isn't magic. It's a gift—of love.* My heart beat wildly, like a dragonfly taking flight.

I couldn't believe it. I looked down at my hand; the ring seemed more mystical and beautiful than ever. I didn't *need* to wear it. My heart swelled and I gasped, blinking back tears. My vision blurred as everything else became crystal clear. I laughed. *So, I really did tell off Cheryl all by myself!*

"Who's there?" Mom asked.

"Oh, it's me, Mom." I wiped the tears from my face.

"Alison, how long have you been there?" Mom wiped her eyes with a tissue.

"You know better than to snoop." Pap's stern voice startled me.

"No. Dad, it's okay. Alli, come and sit," Mom said.

"I heard you talking about moving."

"Your mother will make the right decision, honey. There are lots of things she needs to consider."

"Listen. Pap, Mom. Moving would add another tragic event to our lives. Lisa and I like it here. It doesn't matter where we live. We all carry memories of Dad in our hearts. I heard Mom talk about her ring." I smiled at Mom. "I never even noticed your ring, Mom." My voice cracked. "This house holds many more good memories than bad. I like school. Mom is seeing a counselor, and Lisa's finally doing well in school." I met Pap's stare. "We're going to be okay."

"Well, someone has grown up pretty fast." He chuckled. "With a dang good head on her shoulders."

"You're so much like your father," Mom whispered, shaking her head.

More than you are willing to believe, Mom. I twirled the ring and looked at Pap. "I love having you guys around. It's great when you're here—I just don't want to move."

"No, Dad." Mom sniffed and put her hand on mine. "Alli's right. We're going to stay and make it work here. Why don't you and Mom come once a month or so? We would love to have you."

He nodded thoughtfully and stood up. "Well, it looks like Grandma Claus will be coming to Virginia this year."

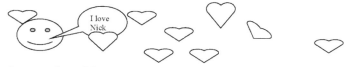

September 22
Dearest Diary,

Do you believe in love at first sight????? I do!!! Yesterday may have been the worst day of my life, but now I understand why I had to let go of Eric. I had to let my heart be open for NICKKKKK KLARRRRKKK.

This is what happened only a few short hours ago:

Mom thought we should go to the mall for a girls' day. She thought (and I agreed) that we should replace Jelly Beans (R.I.P.) with something more sophisticated, say a Coach clutch or something. Of course, that sounded perfect to me!

Once we were at the mall, Mom needed to return a pair of pants she bought for Matt in Macy's, so she gave me five bucks to go to the food court. I walked over there, and sitting at one of the tables, was NICK KLARK. I didn't think much of it; I just kind of waved at him and got in line at Orange Julius. Next thing I knew; there he was standing next to me—two inches away—staring!

It freaked me out to see him so close, so I just said, "Hi." He said, "Hi," and just stood there staring and smiling. I asked him if he was getting a drink or something. (I had to say *some*thing, he was standing so close I was freaking!)

He said, "No. I just wondered if you were going to the play tomorrow night." I told him no. (As if— sit and watch Alli and Eric play lovers?) Then, get this, he stepped even closer to me. (I felt his (French fry-ish in a good way, not bad at all!) breath on me he was so close!)

He said, "That's too bad. I would've been sick to see you in the crowd."

I choked! I didn't know what to say. All of a sudden the lady at the counter wanted to know what I wanted to order. I ordered a small Strawberry Julius (obvi-best drink ever) and then (I don't know what came over me; I just got goose bumps re-thinking this part) I asked Nick if he wanted a drink, my treat, and he ordered a small strawberry too! (His all time fav also!) Then, he wanted to know if he could sit with me.

I said, "Sure." Trying to act cool, but I was freaking! We talked for a couple of minutes and he told me he saw me at the pool last summer and always wanted to talk to me, but was too afraid. He's actually pretty cute and really nice.

Mom walked up and Nick introduced himself to Mom and she was very impressed by his nice manners. He said he hoped I would come to the play, and Mom said I would be there. Mom practically squeezed my arm off while we shopped, talking about what a handsome and polite boy Nick is and blah blah. It was honestly the best time at the mall.

Did I mention that he's pretty cute and really nice?

Chapter 27

Monday night finally arrived and our class stood in the hall—a hyper, giggling mass of red, white and blue T-shirts. I peeked through the door's window to our classroom. Our desks were stacked in the back and lots of grown-ups huddled together in four rows of chairs with knees touching. I saw Grandma, Pap, Mom and Lisa sitting in the second row. My mouth felt like a dried sponge and I walked over to the water fountain. Eric was crouched in the nook beside the fountain and some lockers.

"Hey? Are you okay?" I took a deep breath, trying to calm my voice.

He lifted his head and his face was pale, ill-looking—similar to his expression a few days ago in my yard.

"Eric! What's wrong?"

"Alli. This is going to be a disaster." He put his head in his hands.

"Hey." I said and slid down next to him. "Who cares? You'll be great."

"I don't know all my lines. I don't get this stupid stuff.

Mrs. Nottingham is going to have a stroke."

"You know what Romeo is like though, right?"

He shrugged.

"That's the important part. The words will come to you if you know the feelings behind them. You'll be okay. I'll be there."

"You won't be with me all the time."

"Well, how would you like something to remind you that I will be thinking about you and wishing you good luck?"

He nodded. "Anything from you will help."

I placed the ring in his hand.

"Uh—you want me to wear this?"

"Why don't you put it in your pocket?"

I helped him to his feet. "It will bring you good luck. Trust me."

"Okay everyone. It's time." Mrs. Nottingham said. "Eric, Alli. Where are you?"

"Right here, Mrs. Nottingham." Eric raised his hand limply.

"Come over here, you two. Alli, are you ready? You need to go and stand up on the counter. Be careful of the cardboard balcony, it's very tipsy."

I walked back to the group of kids and saw Margot in her blue T-shirt talking to Nick in his white T-shirt. Our eyes met. She didn't smile, nor did she frown; she just had a sad look in her eyes. I raised my chin and gave a little smile, hoping she might smile back. She rolled her eyes at me and handed Nick a note. *Why is she giving Nick a note? She's not sad about us; she just didn't want to give Nick that note.*

Nothing had changed. She and 3B were still tight. It didn't mean anything when she walked away from Cheryl at my house. There's no way she'd cry over me. I took a deep breath and shook my head. *Pull it together, Juliet!*

"Should I go now?" I asked Mrs. Nottingham.

She peered into the class. "Yes." Her expression became concerned when she glanced at Eric, who seemed a shade paler than before. "Mr. Prinz, are you well?" But then she put her hand up to stop him from answering. "Let me rephrase. Are you going to throw up—this very second?"

He shook his head no.

"Okay, then break a leg." She looked at me. "Both of you."

"I really wish she hadn't said that," Eric whispered.

I gave Eric a little squeeze on his shoulder, and he tried to smile. He was adorable even when he looked as if he might hurl.

I walked into the classroom and the audience hushed. Carefully, I stepped on a chair and then onto the ledge holding the cardboard balcony in front of me.

Mrs. Nottingham walked in front of the classroom and cleared her throat. "Welcome everyone to our rendition of Act II of *Romeo and Juliet*. The students have worked very hard for several weeks getting prepared. Everything you see, from costumes to scenery, has been made by them. So, without further ado, we begin Act II at Scene II, in the Capulets orchard."

I couldn't see Eric, but the crowd turned and looked toward the door. My stomach clenched as I waited for him to start.

"He jests at scars that never felt a wound."

I swallowed hard and stepped out into the middle of the counter, being careful not to touch the wobbly balcony. I didn't look toward Eric; I wasn't supposed to know he was there. I was *supposed* to look toward the back of the room, but instead I peered around the audience. Cheryl Thomas, sitting next to June and Mrs. Williamson looked at me and smiled. *Something's up.* June bounced in her seat next to Cheryl waving like mad. Mom, Lisa, Grandma and Pap sat near-by, beaming up at me.

"But soft! What light through yonder window breaks? It is the east, and Juliet is the sun. Arise, fair sun, and kill the envious moon, who is already sick and pale with grief, be not her maid since she is envious." Eric stopped.

What's happening? I flicked a glance at him and found him gawking at me. *He's gonna barf!*

"Juliet!" He said in a panicky-desperate tone, so I looked at him, completely ignoring Mrs. Nottingham's stage directions.

"The moon looks sick and green. Ah, like liver, and only a fool would wear it. Take it off my lady, my lady love."

What is he saying? It sounded like he wanted me to take off my dress! Those were not his lines. I glanced at Mrs. Nottingham and she looked like she'd just seen a kitten beaten.

Eric continued, "Speak Juliet, speak."

He sounded like he was begging me to say something, *anything*. It wasn't time for me to speak yet! He didn't talk about my eyes being stars or the glove touching my cheek or any of Romeo's lines. I went with it. "Aye me."

"She speaks, oh Juliet, angel." He licked his lips and looked at the audience. "I will paraphrase."

No!

"Juliet, you are an angel to me, I've gazed at your face and surely you are a winged messenger from heaven. Beautiful face, beautiful heart that God placed on that balcony for me to adore."

Dead silence.

What should I do? He stood there staring at me. "Thank you, Romeo."

Mrs. Nottingham ran out and handed Eric her copy of the play. She pointed to the correct line and said, "Here!"

He looked down and said, "*Shall I hear more, or shall I speak at this.*" He'd found the real lines! *Whew.* I knew how to answer these!

Eric kept the copy in front of him and I remembered most of my lines. I wasn't acting when I said to him, "*And I will follow thee my lord throughout the world.*"

Ginny stood on the counter near the curtain and yelled, "Madame!" which was her line, but *not* her stage direction. She was supposed to alert me, not terrify me. I jumped as if I had seen a mouse—which was absolutely not what I was supposed to do— and lost my balance on the ledge. I lunged forward, grabbing the cardboard balcony, and fell with all the grace of an anvil. Imagine what a large dog in an oversized T-shirt might look like if it were getting ready to take a pee. That's what I felt like as I landed on my hands and knees, and I am sure it is what I looked like especially when I let out a whiney, high-pitched *whooooooooo* upon landing.

Eric stepped on the balcony and whispered, "Are you okay?"

"I think so," I whimpered. He grabbed my hand and helped me up.

He gently squeezed my hand, turned to the audience and said, "*I wish you were a bird.*"

I squeezed it back and said, "So do I."

The crowd roared. I giggled and probably turned the color of Eric's red T-shirt. I caught a glimpse of Mom bent over laughing, really laughing. Actually, everyone looked like they were in hysterics except Mrs. Nottingham; she had her hand on her forehead and was leaning on the wall.

I tried to get serious again for Mrs. Nottingham's sake, but it was like laughing in church—once you get going it's really hard to stop. Giggling, I said, "*Good night, good night, parting is such sweet sorrow, I shall say good night till it be morrow.*" I walked off stage right, where Mrs. Nottingham looked quite pale and a little scary.

"Are you okay?" She grabbed my shoulders.

"Yeah. Just embarrassed."

Her face softened into a smile. "Thank goodness." She let out a sigh and hugged me very tight. "Alli, you've got some comic chops and resilient bones."

Eric finished his lines and Mrs. Nottingham dashed out, pulled the sheet across the crumpled balcony and said, "Get Friar Laurence's cell out here!"

I gauged how well the rest of the play went by Mrs. Nottingham's face. The crease in her forehead seemed to soften a little as each scene passed. Finally, Nick, as Friar

Lawrence, finished his lines when Eric—I mean, Romeo—
and I were supposed to get married. I thought everyone
could see my beating heart through my blue T-shirt as I
gazed into Eric's eyes and pretended, just a little bit. He
smiled at me. Deliriously happy, I hoped that Cheryl was
getting an eye full of this. She was—and smiling! *Something
very weird was up—unsettling is what Dad would have called
it.*

The audience applauded and stood as Mrs. Nottingham
announced the cast. She introduced me after Eric as, "Our
fair Juliet, Alison Collins." I stepped in front and bowed.
The crowd cheered, but I recognized Pap's whistle above all
the other noise. I enjoyed a warm, happy feeling. Mom
smiled and wiped a tear from her cheek. *Was she proud of me?*

Cheryl politely clapped when Margot was introduced,
but went crazy yelling, "Yahoo!" when Nick stepped out and
bowed. *Oh, no. She's gonna trick Nick somehow.*

Red, white and blue T-shirted ninth graders sprinkled
into the crowd. Eric slipped his pinky finger in mine and
smiled. Tender warmth ignited my heart like flint hitting
stone. It sent sparks so strong that I shuddered when I smiled
back at him. Over his shoulder, I watched Cheryl stand up
holding a white carnation. She glanced over and met my
stare with a soft smile as she headed toward Nick. *Oh no!*

Lisa wrapped her arms around my waist. "You were really
funny, Alli."

"Yeah, I guess it was funny."

"I'll be right back." Eric let go of my finger.

"Okay." My gaze stayed glued to Cheryl as she handed

Nick the flower, looking shy and embarrassed. Some evil was about to unfold, I just knew it. This was too weird, even for her. Nick took a note out of his pocket. *What is going on? Did Margot deliver a note from Cheryl? Is this for real—Cheryl likes Nick? I don't get it.*

Eric returned with a bouquet of purple flowers for me. "I asked my mom to bring these for you. You were great."

"Great? Falling off the balcony?"

"Well, you kept the attention off of me." He laughed and then became serious. "No, honestly, Alli. You were great."

His green eyes were more beautiful than the flowers. "Thank you. These are gorgeous."

"Eric. What a gentleman." Mom said as she walked up with Grandma and Pap right behind her.

"Alli, you were the star of the show," Grandma said.

"You were both wonderful." Mom kissed me on the cheek. "Eric, where's your mom? I'd like to tell her how wonderful you and your brother have been."

"Oh, you really don't have to do that."

"Don't you think we should introduce ourselves? For Pete's Sake, you two just got married." Mom raised one eyebrow at me.

Mom!

"Oh. That's funny." Eric pointed over the crowd. "She's over there, in the brown jacket."

"Mom, Dad, Lisa, come with me." Mom winked at me. "See you at the car in a few minutes."

"Okay," I said. *Jeesh. How embarrassing!*

Cheryl giggled with Nick.

"Hey, look at that." I pointed over to them.

"Wow. I guess I don't take long to get over," Eric said.

"Can you believe that?"

"Uh, yeah," he said. "Cheryl's desperate for people to like her."

"Like her? Cheryl Thomas? She's sure got a weird way of showing it."

"Well, for as long as I've known her, she always begging to hang out with Travis, Matt and me when we're playing ball and stuff. She's always alone when I see her. She's probably jealous of you."

"Jealous?"

"Yeah. I think so."

I sniffed the flowers trying to hide the giddy joy that bubbled up and contorted my face as if I'd gulped a really fizzy soda.

"How about I walk you to your car, my fair Juliet?"

I sucked in my cheeks, trying to force my ecstatic glee into something like normal, polite happiness. "That would be nice."

There was still light in the sky, and it was a balmy. I heard locusts in the distance.

"It won't be this warm much longer," Eric said.

"Well, it's really nice tonight." *Did we have to talk about the weather?*

He reached into his pocket and held out my ring. "Thanks for the ring. It didn't help too much."

"Did it help you remember that I was thinking of you and wishing you luck?"

"Well, I was hoping it would help me remember my lines."

"It wasn't supposed to do that. It was supposed to remind you that I like you no matter what, even if you don't remember your lines."

Eric placed the ring in my palm and my fingers automatically curled around his hand. He leaned in and his soft lips met mine, but this time he didn't hesitate. This time, it was a real honest-to-gosh, curl-your-toes, knees-buckling type of kiss. He stepped back, "That kiss helped more than any ring ever could."

What ring? I thought, dazed.

Pap came out of the school door and I saw Grandma, Mom and Lisa through the glass door about to step outside.

"Here comes my family."

"Well, I guess I should get going and find my folks. I'll see ya later, okay?" He kissed my cheek.

I looked over and saw Lisa's eyes widen as she clapped her hand over her mouth. I grinned. "I'll see ya."

"Ready?" Mom walked up to the car.

I walked around to the other side of the car waiting for Mom to unlock the door, and you're not going to believe this—a dragonfly landed on my bouquet. Seriously! My mouth gaped open and I stared at it until the *click* of the car door scared it away. It floated away in the night air. "Goodbye," I told it softly. "And thank you." Just in case.

Chapter 28

Everyone was eating breakfast as I entered the kitchen. Grandma and Pap's suitcases were ready to go by the door.

"Alli, remember you have an appointment at Dr. Blume's this morning." Mom stood up with her coffee mug and headed toward the sink.

"Oh, yeah. What time?" I never remember my orthodontist appointments. As far as I was concerned, my braces were a permanent fixture in my mouth, forgettable in all ways.

"This morning at nine. I'll pick you up after first period."

"Can I just miss first period? We never do anything in Mrs. Moore's class."

"Nothing?" Grandma said.

"Not really." It was really shocking how lame Consumer Science was. So far, all Mrs. Moore had taught me was what not to do in the kitchen.

"Okay." Mom headed for the refrigerator.

"Janet," Grandma said in a sharp tone.

"Mom, please." She sighed. "It's easier for everyone."

"Thanks." I grabbed a bagel.

"Dad, did you pack the sandwiches I made for you?"

"Yes. We have everything. Now give us a kiss. I want to get on the road before the highway's jammed." Pap headed toward the suitcases. "Let's make this quick and painless, Grandma."

We hugged and kissed our way to the driveway. Grandma buckled in and waved at us as we yelled, "Bye!" Margot walked up the sidewalk as we watched their car disappear. She stopped at the bottom of the driveway.

"Want to walk together?" Her hands were jammed in her pockets, her shoulders pinched toward her ears.

"I'm not going on the bus. Got an ortho appointment this morning."

"Oh. Well, do you have a second?" She wouldn't look at me. Instead, she kicked an ant hill on the edge of the sidewalk.

Oh jeez. Don't look nervous. Lisa looked at me with wide anxious eyes as she held Mom's hand and walked back into the house. I nodded slightly at her and raised my hand faking a calm *it's okay* sign. "Yeah, sure." I stared at ants that were probably screaming terrified in their little ant voices from the shoe-shaped meteor that just ruined their very existence. I took a deep breath fighting my instinct to run away like the ants.

"Alli, I'm sorry." She stared at the scurrying ants, seemingly oblivious to her power of destruction. Something dripped onto the ant hill.

Do I see tears? "Yeah?"

Tears streamed down her face. "I messed up."

"What are you talking about?" Clearly, she wasn't referring to the ant hill.

"The way I've treated you." She sniffed. "The way I've been treating you, starting that day I came over to your house to read that journal. I really lost it that day. I couldn't believe how bad it felt to walk into your house. You know, since your dad's been gone."

"Is that what this is all about?" Margot wasn't fighting for control; she was waving a white flag. I hadn't put mine out yet.

"I don't know. I really didn't like the way everything was. Your mom—the house—everything—was different."

Tell me about it. "Why would you be mean to me, though?"

"I don't know." She wiped her face with the back of her hand and shook her head. "I don't know—scared maybe? This whole thing has really shaken me up. I thought somehow things would be just the same."

"Like he was still here or something?" *Just like I waited for him to walk off the Metro bus every day for a week after he died? I prayed he would walk off the bus just like he used to, like everyone else's parent did, like he did hundreds of times before.*

"No, no. I don't mean that. Well, I don't know, maybe. It's just so horrible, Alli." She put her hands over her face and sobbed. We were still standing at the bottom of my driveway.

"Do you want to come inside?"

She shook her head. "Remember?" Snot dribbled onto her lip, but there was no way I was going to say anything. "Remember how—every t-time I came over t-to your house?"

She could barely catch her breath in between her gasps. "Your dad always called me..." She mumbled, "*Beautiful?*"

I heard her.

"I believed him." She put her hands over her face. "I loved your dad, Alli. I really miss him. It was easier to hate you." She wiped the stream of snot at the bottom of her nose. "I know that sounds so lame. You were so lucky. I've always been so jealous of you because of you and your dad. I can't believe how awful I've been." She was really bawling. I'd never seen this before. Ever.

I got it. I did have the greatest dad. Her real dad was a bum and even though Bill adopted her, it just wasn't the same.

"I miss you s-so much."

My bottom lip quivered, and I clenched my teeth to try and keep myself from falling apart. I was ready to wave my white flag, but she wasn't finished.

"Remember at your dad's funeral?"

"Uh huh."

"Remember, I said something to you?"

I sniffed. "Yeah. I couldn't hear you."

She broke into sobs again. "I tried to tell you, 'He always called me beautiful.'"

My heart melted. "It sucks, doesn't it?" I hugged her tight, wrapping her in my white flag of truce.

"Alli." Margot stepped away from me. "Nothing has sucked more than not having you around."

I poked her in the side, giggling with awkward happiness and relief. "Bosom buddies?"

She looked down and chuckled. "Yeah. That would be awesome."

"Well, I'll see ya later. I don't think I'm going to be in English, but save me a spot on the bus on the way home?"

"Sounds good." She smiled. "Actually, sounds great."

****

Mom and I walked into Dr. Blume's waiting room and saw Mrs. Thomas filling out paper work.

What's she doing here?

"Shirley," Mom said. "You got an appointment quickly."

What's Mom talking about?

"Hi Janet. Alli."

"Uh, hi, Mrs. Thomas." I nudged Mom and whispered, "What's going on?"

Mom sat next to me and said in a low voice, "I called Mrs. Thomas again on Saturday to thank her for Matt's help and she asked me about our orthodontist. I gave her Dr. Blume's number."

"For Matt?" *No way would that perfect mouth need braces.*

"No. For Cheryl." A flushing sound came from the bathroom and out walked 3B herself.

Great. This is going to ruin a perfect morning.

"Oh, hi Mrs. Collins. Alli."

"Hi," I said.

Mrs. Thomas walked up to the receptionist with a question about the paperwork. I heard her say, "No, no. That's not it," and she turned to Mom. "Janet? Can I steal you for a minute?"

I kept my face in an old *Seventeen* magazine looking at swimsuits that would have flattered my figure last summer. Mom walked to the counter, and I felt Cheryl's stare from three seats away.

"Alli?"

Ignore. Ignore. Focus on the bust-enhancing bikini top.

"Alli?" She got up and sat in the seat next to me.

I shifted in my seat. "Oh. Hey." I tried to sound surprised.

"Great job last night. You were really great."

"Thanks." *I hate those racerback tops.*

"So, you and Eric are official, huh?"

That's it. I closed the magazine and looked at her. She really didn't seem too scary today. "Why are you talking to me?" I went for it. "You treat me like dirt forever, and now all of a sudden you want to be buddies? On Saturday morning, you made it pretty clear you didn't want Eric hanging out with me. Remember Saturday morning, Cheryl? You called me a spastic loser, I believe? And you called my whole family nuts?" I pointed to Mom.

"I'm sorry about the whole spaz business." She looked at her hands and lowered her voice. "You called me pathetic and you were right. I was."

What is going on today? First Margot's confession and now this? I looked down at my ring and shook my head. *Very strange.*

"I'm getting braces. Time to make some big changes."

"Oh." *Would it be rude to agree one hundred percent?*

"Yeah. Stopping bad habits and starting a new relationship."

"With Nick Klark?"

"Yeah. Nick." It was the first time I have ever seen her with a wide, genuine smile. It made her look very different, maybe even a little goofy.

Jeez, so this is what 3B is really like? I giggled.

"What's so funny?" Cheryl asked, but not in a mean way, but more like she was afraid I was laughing at *her*.

"Nothing. It's just been a weird day."

The nurse called my name. Mom looked at me and nodded, letting me know it was okay. She was still talking with the receptionist and Mrs. Thomas.

Twenty minutes later I walked out into the waiting room and found Mom all by herself. "How'd it go?" she asked as we walked to the car.

"Normal. Do you have any Tylenol? My mouth's killing me. Dr. Blume told me I needed to brush my teeth better."

"How many times have I told you that?" Mom fished a couple of Tylenol out of her purse and started the car.

"How'd it go with Mrs. Thomas?"

"She was very confused. I guess Mr. Thomas usually takes care of all the family's paperwork. It felt kind of good to help her out. I saw you talking to Cheryl. How'd that go?"

"Okay. She said that I was really good last night. Then— you're not going to believe it—she told me she was sorry about calling me spaz all last year."

"Well, you were wonderful last night. I'm glad she said she was sorry. That was pretty mean of her." Mom pulled up to school. "See ya later, okay?"

"Yeah, see ya." *Pretty mean? That's like saying ice is kinda cold.* Mom would never get it like Dad did.

****

"Hey Alli!" I heard Margot's voice as I stepped onto the bus to go home. She patted the seat next to her. "Here, sit here."

I looked at her and saw Cheryl wave shyly at me from the back of the bus. I raised my fingers a little to acknowledge her wave.

"Hey. How was the orthodontist?" Her tone was friendly, just like the good old days.

"O-M-G. You're not going to believe who I saw there."

"Who?"

"Cheryl Thomas."

"No." She looked back toward Cheryl. "Why didn't you text me?"

"I didn't have a chance. My mom talked to me the whole way to school.

"What was she doing there?"

"She's getting braces. And get this—she apologized for calling me a spaz!"

"Seriously?" She looked back again.

"Yup." I turned toward Margot and lowered my voice a little. "Did you give Nick Klark a note from Cheryl last night?"

"Yes. She begged me to. She called me on Sunday night, all hyper, telling me how she met him at the mall and yada yada, he's really nice—blah, blah. Can you believe after all the crap she put us both through about Eric, now she suddenly likes Nick? Just like that...boom, new show in town." She pointed to the ring that sparkled at us from where I gripped the seat in front. "Everything has been very weird since you found that ring, Alli."

"I wasn't wearing the ring on Saturday."

"Seriously?"

"Seriously."

We both glanced back at Cheryl, who raised her eyebrows at us and lifted her chin in a friendly way. *Maybe we should ask her to join us? It sure seems like that's what she wants..*

The bus lurched to a halt and let us out. As we walked away, I heard a "Hey, Alli, Margot. Wait." I turned around and saw Cheryl with her hand in the air. "Can I walk with you guys?"

Did I call it or what?

I looked at Margot, and she shrugged.

"Sure," I said.

The sidewalk was just wide enough for the three of us to walk together. The sun broke through a cloud and made filtered streams of light that hit the trees like a spot-light on their dusty red tops. Fall was on its way. Even in the chill of the afternoon air, I glowed from inside—filled with warmth and contentment for the first time in a long time.

I looked down at my ring and smiled. Magic? I thought so.

The gift of love is pretty powerful stuff.

If you enjoyed *Alli's Gift*, please give it a five star rating on Amazon. These ratings are an independent publishers tip jar. It takes a few seconds and means so much. You can easily rate *Alli's Gift* by going to
www.kathleendenniston.com

Made in the USA
Middletown, DE
08 December 2017